SURVIVAL

TITANIC
APRIL 14, 1912

K. DUEY AND K. A. BALE

For Ged —

Merry Christmas!

Katy

ALADDIN PAPERBACKS

FOR THE WOMEN WHO TAUGHT US THE MEANING OF COURAGE:

ERMA L. KOSANOVICH
KATHERINE B. BALE
MARY E. PEERY

———————

First Aladdin Paperbacks edition January 1998

Aladdin Paperbacks
An imprint of Simon & Schuster
Children's Publishing Division
1230 Avenue of the Americas
New York, NY 10020

Library of Congress Cataloging-in-Publication Data
Duey, Kathleen
Shipwreck : the Titanic, 1912 / K. Duey and K.A. Bale.
—1st Aladdin Paperbacks ed.
p.   cm.—(Survival! ; bk. 1)
Summary: During the final hours aboard the Titanic on her ill-fated voyage in 1912, Gavin and Karolina attempt to help others and by so doing learn something about themselves.
ISBN 0-689-81311-2 (pbk.)
1. Titanic (Steamship)—Juvenile Fiction. [1. Titanic (Steamship)—Fiction. 2. Shipwrecks—Fiction. 3. Survival—Fiction. 4. Ocean liners—Fiction.]
I. Bale, Karen A. II. Title. III. Series: Duey, Kathleen. Survival! ; bk. 1.
PZ7.D8694Sh   1998
[Fic]—dc21   97-38594
CIP   AC

CHAPTER ONE

Gavin Reilly stood on the boat deck of the *Titanic*, his eyes closed tightly. He gripped the handrail and counted to ten. Then he opened his eyes again. He had to get over this. He *had* to get used to looking out over the open water. After a few dizzying seconds, he turned landward, gulping huge breaths of the cool air. He stared at the coastline and the green hills above Queenstown, Ireland. This was ridiculous. He had been swimming since he was a baby. He had never been afraid of water in his life.

"Are you all right?"

Gavin looked up to see a girl with light brown hair, and a scattering of freckles across the bridge of her nose. She looked concerned. Her accent, broadly American, sounded brash and rude.

"Are you sick?"

Gavin shook his head. There was no way to explain what was wrong with him. He didn't really understand it himself. "I'm fine," he said, staring back at the shoreline.

The town's docks were all too small for the *Titanic*, so the enormous liner had been anchored two miles offshore. Passengers, goods, and mailbags were being brought out to her. Gavin watched the tenders and bumboats scuttling back and forth. The *Ireland* was not a small boat, but it looked like a toy beside the *Titanic*. The *America* stood off a little distance, waiting its turn to unload.

Gavin watched a bumboat come alongside. Most of them were loaded with Irish goods. The first-class nabobs and their finely dressed wives would have their chance to buy Irish linen and lace, even if they couldn't go ashore.

Gavin glanced sideways. The girl was still standing nearby, but she was looking out to sea

now, her hair blowing in the wind. Gavin wanted more than anything to turn and face the
open water, but he knew he couldn't. He
moved a little ways away from the girl, hoping
she wouldn't follow.

Gavin leaned against the metal railing. The
familiar green curve of the south Irish coast was
less than two miles away over the water. He
stared at Queenstown with its narrow streets
and closely packed buildings. He sighed.

The hills behind the town were so green,
they reminded him of his home outside Belfast.
He could imagine his brothers and sisters tend-
ing the potato patch in the high pasture. Sean's
voice would be ringing out over little Katie's
giggles. Gavin could almost see her, freckled
and pink-faced. Liam would be arguing with
Mary. The little ones would be with Mother at
home, lined up on her cot for noontime nap.
Gavin felt the now-familiar physical ache that
always accompanied thoughts of his family. He
might never see them again.

"Are you ill?" the girl asked.

Gavin glanced at her and shook his head,

then pointedly turned his back. He forced himself to look out to sea. The cold gray water stretched all the way to the horizon. He wasn't sure why it bothered him so much. Everyone agreed the *Titanic* was unsinkable. That very morning they had run a full dress rehearsal emergency; alarms sounding, they had closed all the watertight doors.

Gavin had been so determined to get a position on the *Titanic* that he had traveled to Southampton, lied about his age, and stood in line with several hundred others to be interviewed. Conor's letters from New York had set him dreaming of a different life. Like all older brothers, Conor wanted him to have opportunities, too. Their mother had lit a candle for Conor the day he had sailed for America. Now she would light two every Sunday. The idea of the candles made Gavin feel a sharp stab of homesickness.

"I didn't mean to intrude," the girl said apologetically. He glanced at her, about to apologize for his own rudeness, but she had already turned away.

He watched her walk past the gigantic funnel that jutted up at an angle from the deck. The other three were real and spouted black smoke when the *Titanic* was underway. This one was fake, nothing more than a huge air vent. Still, like the others, it was anchored with thick steel cables. Gavin saw the girl start down the steep stairs toward the third-class promenade.

"Hey, Gavin! You'd better get back down to the galley." Lionel's voice startled him. The tall, blond-haired boy dropped onto one of the wooden benches along the handrail. "Mr. Hughes will see you slacking, and they'll be booting you off. That would shame your roommates, you know."

Gavin grinned. "I would hate to do that."

"Well, Harry and I would be shamed at any rate. I'm not sure Wallace has it in him."

They both laughed. "I've only been up here a few minutes," Gavin said. "I needed fresh air."

Lionel shrugged. "Are you seasick? At anchor? It's going to be like sailing a whole city across the Atlantic, Gavin. She barely rolls at all."

Gavin shot one more glance at the open water and felt his stomach tighten. "I'd better get started washing the new potatoes. First class is going to have them boiled *parmentier.*"

"Work hard and you can end up a first-class steward like me." Lionel stood up straight, clowning, squaring his shoulders in exaggerated pride. "I have to go down to the dining room to deliver a message."

"I'll go down with you," Gavin said, getting to his feet.

Together they headed toward the second-class entrance. Gavin reached out to open the door. Side by side they started down the long stairway. Their steps were timed to a rhythmic patter that kept them moving downward at almost a running pace. Lionel had taught Gavin how to run the stairs like this and he shot him a grin of approval. "You're getting good."

Gavin grinned back, feeling better.

As they descended past the windows of the Palm Court, he saw the first-class passengers seated in the elaborately decorated garden room. There were a few men onboard who were so wealthy, their clothing had probably cost more than it took to feed Gavin's family for a whole year. He had seen one woman wearing a necklace of diamonds so big, they shot glitters across the room.

On the B-deck landing, Gavin could smell the heavy scent of tobacco coming from the second-class smoking room. Lionel lifted one hand to cover his nose and mouth. Gavin nodded. First-class was the worst—expensive cigars had a pungent odor that clung to the very walls.

As they went deeper into the ship, Gavin felt his nervousness subside a little. Down here, the *Titanic* was much like a grand hotel. It was easier to forget the deep gray water that would soon separate him from his family and from the farm where he had lived his whole life.

"What time are you off Saturday night?" Lionel asked.

Gavin grabbed the handrail as they rounded the landing on C-deck. "After cleanup. Around ten."

"Come up to the first-class dining room—

it's empty by then, and a few of us are going to have a card game."

Gavin glanced at the side of Lionel's face, then looked back at the stairs. "I've been coming up here." He pointed at the second-class library as they started downward again.

"You're going to read? When you could be playing poker?"

Gavin smiled and nodded. "I have to get to New York with all my pay. I can't expect my brother to support me."

Lionel slowed as they reached D-deck. "Come up if you change your mind. You can just sit with us; you don't have to play."

"I will, thanks."

Gavin watched as Lionel went into the first-class dining saloon. Through the open door Gavin saw that the room was still pretty full. The stewards were just beginning to clear away dirty dishes. Lionel's rakish grin disappeared, and his face became a mask of politeness as he turned and bent to whisper discreetly to a woman in a green silk gown.

Gavin shook his head as he pulled the door

closed and turned to cross the landing. Going into the first-class pantry, he walked fast, rounding the corner by the neatly stacked crates of Waken & McLaughlin wine. The roast cook and one of the confectioners came through the galley door ahead of him. He stopped and turned sideways to let them pass. Neither man acknowledged his presence.

Gavin watched them walk away. He wasn't like Lionel. It was hard for him to smile at people who were rude to him, whether they were crew or passengers. He hurried into the galley, wishing he had been hired on as a dining room steward. They had it easier. A half hour after the last passenger left the dining saloons, the stewards would be changing the white tablecloths and setting the tables for the next meal. Then they would have a break.

"Hey! Gavin!"

Gavin turned to see Harry making his way across the crowded galley. His sharp-featured face was smudged with flour. He was already developing the short-strided, agile walk necessary to avoid collisions in the crowded, busy room.

Cooking never ceased here, except for a few hours in the middle of the night. The bakers began at three in the morning. The cooks started preparing breakfast early, then began lunch before the breakfast dishes were cleared. Dinner preparation sometimes started a day in advance, all the meals overlapping—only the chefs understood the schedule.

"Where have you been off to?" Harry asked, dodging a pantryman carrying an enormous, bloody roast. "You missed a chance to watch the pastry chef make éclairs."

Gavin shrugged. Harry wanted to be a chef someday and he rarely left the galley. "I went up for air," Gavin told him. "I just like to see the sky once in a while."

Harry nodded vaguely, turning when the sauce chef bellowed out an order. Then his eyes focused on Gavin again. "What do you have to do now?"

Gavin made a face. "Wash a hundred and twenty pounds of new potatoes." Harry laughed, and Gavin pretended to take a swing at him. "It isn't funny. I hate the new potatoes worst of all. I can't even use the wire brushes because the skins tear so easily."

Harry grinned over his shoulder as he walked away. "Better you than me."

Gavin went to his basin. The pantrymen had already brought in the bags. He stared at the lettering. Whoever Charles Papas was, he sure raised a lot of potatoes.

"When do we raise anchor?" someone yelled behind him.

"Soon," the answer came. "Less than half an hour."

Gavin's throat tightened. There was no turning back now.

CHAPTER TWO

"Are you coming, Aunt Rose?" Karolina asked impatiently. She turned a page in her father's Bible. She wasn't really reading. It just made her feel close to her parents to have the big leather-covered book in her hands. Her father had used it every night to work on his sermons, or just to study.

"Don't rush me," Aunt Rose said.

Karolina set down the Bible and scooted to the edge of her berth, her legs extending almost to the middle of the tiny third-class stateroom. The toes of her shoes brushed the white porcelain of the exposed commode. Out in the corridor a man began to argue with his wife. In seconds, they were both shouting in a language Karolina had never heard before.

Aunt Rose closed the door, then sank onto her berth. "Listen to that. I told you third class would be interesting."

"I've traveled in steerage before, Aunt Rose. Papa thought paying for anything but third class was a waste of money." She shook her head. "Are you ready?"

"Hold on, Little Miss Impatience." Aunt Rose bent to straighten her stocking seam.

Karolina tapped one foot and picked up the Bible again. There was a tiny packet of pressed violet petals that her mother had put between the pages long ago. Without warning, Karolina's eyes flooded with tears, and she blinked them away. She was finished with crying. Nothing was going to bring back Mama and Papa.

"Stateroom number fifty-five," Aunt Rose said, gesturing at their little cabin. "It certainly is spacious."

"A regular palace," Karolina agreed, grateful that Aunt Rose had not noticed her tears. She pointed at the huge pipe that ran across the ceiling, then disappeared into the wall. "Fancy decor, you must admit. I bet first-class passengers don't have to shove their bags beneath their berths in order to get to the commode." Karolina sighed.

"And I am sure they have more baths than we do," Aunt Rose complained. "Two for seven hundred of us seems a bit skimpy, don't you think?"

Karolina nodded, arching her brows and waiting. When Aunt Rose got going, she kept going.

"Mrs. John Jacob Astor probably has armoires and wardrobes—and a maid to tend each one," Aunt Rose said, smiling.

"She's pregnant, I hear," Karolina told her.

Aunt Rose frowned. "He left a perfectly good woman for that little chippy."

Karolina smiled. Aunt Rose loved to gossip about people she would never meet. "Can we go up now?"

"I don't want to be out in a cold wind for too long," Aunt Rose said, settling her hat over her thick gray hair. She readjusted a hairpin, tucking a stray strand back into her bun.

"There's a common room upstairs," Karolina said, pushing her father's Bible beneath her pillow. "You can stay inside there if you want to."

Aunt Rose nodded. "I'll follow you. After all, you're the one who figured out the alleys in Southampton. If it had been up to me, we would have missed the boat."

Karolina opened the narrow door, stepping back. Then she peered into the corridor. It was still crowded and noisy, and a hundred unfamiliar smells assaulted her nostrils as she started up the narrow corridor, talking over her shoulder. "We take the stairs up to D-deck. The third-class general room is there. There are lifts, someone said, up in second class. I don't know where, exactly."

"I'll be fine on the stairs, Karolina. I'll just stop and rest if I have to," Aunt Rose said. She pulled in a long breath, and Karolina could hear the tiny wheeze that meant her asthma was bothering her.

Karolina turned left down the corridor. There were stairs straight across from their room, but the door was always locked. It was impossible to tell where the stairs led, but Karolina was pretty sure they opened onto the second-class promenade just above. Aunt Rose said the door was probably locked to keep the steerage passengers from bothering the first- and second-class ticket holders.

Karolina stopped once to let an elderly couple pass by, then again when a little blond-haired girl darted into the passageway ahead of them. Many of the room doors were open, and families sat on their berths, passing the time.

It was impossible not to look into some of the rooms as they passed. Karolina heard so many different languages that it made her feel silly—how could there be so many words that she couldn't understand?

"It's too hot." Aunt Rose said it flatly from behind her.

"It is," Karolina agreed. She rounded a corner and pointed. "Up there. See the landing?"

"Good. Just let me catch my breath for a few seconds."

When Aunt Rose was ready, Karolina started up the stairs behind four young men who were laughing at some joke. With every step, she imagined that she could feel little threads of cool air brushing her face. The young men in front of them began to climb faster and faster, racing each other. Karolina heard a woman's voice raised in protest as they overtook a family dressed in loose white clothing. A second later, the boys were out of sight.

The electric fixtures high on the walls cast semicircles of light on the stairs.

"How much farther?"

Karolina stopped to let Aunt Rose catch her breath again. "The general room is right up there." Karolina pointed at the landing above them. "I want to go outside."

"I think I will, too," Aunt Rose agreed, stepping aside for a pregnant woman who was struggling upward carrying a wide-eyed toddler.

After a few moments, Karolina began climbing again, threading her way through the constant stream of people. On the landing, she opened the heavy door that led into the third-class general room. The benches were lined with people. One family had brought a basket and had spread food out on brightly colored cloths on the floor.

"Where does that one go?" Aunt Rose said, pointing at a second door.

Karolina shook her head. "I don't know." She crossed the landing and opened the door. Through a haze of bluish smoke, Karolina saw men grouped around long tables. A white-haired man smoking a long-stemmed pipe frowned at them, making a shooing motion with his hand.

Karolina stepped back. "How can they stand it?"

Aunt Rose shook her head. "Tobacco smoke makes it impossible for me to breathe." She coughed a little, and Karolina shut the door.

"Excuse . . . please," a man said, startling Karolina into turning around. He pulled a thick cigar from his pocket and waved it back and forth, obviously trusting pantomime more than his command of English. Karolina stepped out of his way and saw Aunt Rose smile as the man went past them. "Handsome," she whispered.

Karolina shook her head. Aunt Rose thought

most men under fifty were handsome, or nice, or sincere, or something that made them sound attractive.

"Come on, now," Karolina teased her. "He's likely married and has four children."

"You're probably right," Aunt Rose teased back. "And his wife is beautiful, intelligent, and twenty years younger than I am."

"You're not that old." Karolina pushed open the doors that led out onto the third-class promenade. It was a small deck, open to the sky. A wave of fresh sea air washed over her. "I could make the whole trip up here." She stood for a few seconds, blinking in the bright sunlight.

Looking toward the bow of the ship, there were two or three decks rising above the promenade, each one a little smaller, like the layers of a wedding cake. There were narrow steps leading up to the first one. Karolina had taken them to get to the boat deck. She wondered if the boy who looked so seasick had gotten any better.

Aunt Rose walked out from beneath the overhang that sheltered the doors. Karolina followed her onto the promenade. She turned in a slow circle, the wind lifting her hair. Aunt Rose was holding her hat on with one hand. "You'll have to start braiding that mane of yours or you'll never manage to comb out the tangles."

Karolina giggled. "You know what they call that?" She pointed toward the stern. "The poop deck."

Aunt Rose rolled her eyes. "You must be teasing."

Karolina shook her head, and they both laughed. "Look," she said, pointing. An enormous wooden pole rose from one of the higher decks, slanting upward. It was anchored to the ship with heavy steel cables that glinted in the sun. On either side of it, huge white cargo hoists lay still like long-necked metallic birds. Each one rested on a white tripod of steel posts. "Do you know what it's for?"

Aunt Rose shook her head. "There are no sails, so it isn't a mast or—"

"Come back!"

Karolina turned to see a dark-haired little boy running toward them. His head was thrown back and he was laughing, obviously delighted to be outside where there was enough room to play. His mother was still close to the stair landing, her arms full of a baby wrapped in blankets. She looked frantic. "Stop him! Stop him, please?"

It took Karolina a moment to separate the woman's words from the sounds of the water and the wind. Once she understood, she sprinted toward the boy. He saw her coming and veered, running faster and giggling. He dodged around the steel supports of one of the cargo hoists.

"Come back here," Karolina called. "Your mother is worried about you."

The little boy squealed and ducked away, circling a piece of machinery. She lunged at him and stepped on the hem of her own skirt. She managed to recover her balance, but not before he had gotten past her.

"Davey Austin, you stand still!" his mother shouted.

Davey didn't even slow down. While Karolina was fighting her wind-billowed skirt, he clambered onto the steep stairs that led to the deck above. Still giggling, he made his way upward so fast that by the time Karolina caught up with him, he was almost at the top. She scooped him up, hooking her arm around his belly. He shrieked in delight, wriggling to get away.

"David Joseph Austin! You come down here now!"

"Be careful, Karolina, watch your step," Aunt Rose called.

Karolina managed to keep Davey under her arm as she carefully descended the steps. At the bottom, Davey squirmed away, sliding out of her grasp. She nearly cried out, but he ran straight for his mother. Holding two fistfuls of her skirt, he tried to hide from Karolina. His chin jutted forward in serious concentration, and Aunt Rose laughed. Karolina shook her head.

"Thank you, dear," Davey's mother said. "I can barely keep track of him today. He is so cooped up down below."

Karolina made a face at Davey when he

peeked at her. He ducked back behind his mother. "I feel that way, too."

"We all do, dear," the mother said, shifting her infant from one arm to the other. "My name is Emily Austin."

"Rose Greene," Aunt Rose said, dropping a mock curtsy. "And this is my niece, Karolina Truman." She bent forward, holding on to her hat with one hand. "And how do you do, Master Davey?" Karolina smiled as Davey hid again at the sound of his own name.

Emily tugged her skirt straight and kissed her baby's cheek. "My husband is in Chicago. Davey, Rebecca, and I will be taking the train west from New York. And you two?"

Karolina glanced at Aunt Rose, then answered. "We're going to New York City. My Aunt Iris lives there, and we are going to stay with her until we can get on our feet."

At Emily's puzzled look, Rose smoothed her skirt, then cleared her throat. "My niece's parents were both killed in England, so I went over to bring her home."

Karolina looked aside. She hated it when

Aunt Rose told people about the accident. Now, after nearly two months, she sometimes stopped thinking about her parents. Why did Aunt Rose have to bring it up with strangers?

" . . . and I cannot seem to get used to the idea that they are gone," Aunt Rose was saying. "I miss Violet so much."

"Violet?"

Karolina stared at the deck above them, knowing what her aunt was about to say.

"Mother named us all for flowers that she loved—Rose, Violet, and Iris."

The constant vibration of the huge engines increased a little. Then, from somewhere above them, Karolina could hear shouted orders. She turned to look. Up on the poop deck, there were several men in dark uniforms. Two of them carried binoculars. They stood up from the bench they had been sitting upon and walked to the railing. Karolina listened to the engines throbbing below decks.

Merry laughter made Karolina turn and look at the highest deck. Women dressed in billowing silk, and men in well-cut suits lined the railings.

One woman held a dog with silken white fur and black button eyes.

"Look at them," Emily said softly. "There's more money up there than in a New York bank."

Aunt Rose nodded. "Mr. and Mrs. Straus are onboard. They own Macy's, you know. It's the nicest department store I have ever been in. Mr. Guggenheim is up there, too. And of course the Astors—"

"One of the stewards told me an incredible story," Emily interrupted her. She shifted her baby again. Davey had let go of his mother's skirts and was sitting beside them now, playing with his shoe buttons. "He said there's a fifteen-year-old girl up there who gets seven thousand five hundred dollars' allowance every year—just for school and her clothes. She's an heiress of some kind."

Karolina looked at the high deck, at the smiling men and women who stood upon it, then back out at the gray water. She didn't care about the fancy people. And she didn't care if she ever saw Ireland or England again, either.

Maybe back in America she would be able to stop reimagining the automobile accident, stop crying every night. Aunt Rose said it would just take time for her to get over missing her parents so much.

"I'd give anything to see the inside of one of the first-class staterooms," Emily said, leaning close to Aunt Rose.

"Probably have a better chance of being struck by lightning in a forest," Aunt Rose answered.

"Probably," Emily agreed. "But I'd sure love the chance. I'd figure out a way if I didn't have these two." She reached down to touch Davey's dark curly hair.

"What do you mean?" Karolina asked.

"There are no iron bars on the stairways, are there? I'd wait for a quiet time, then I'd just go have a look."

"And get thrown out?" Aunt Rose demanded, laughing.

Karolina walked away from them, glancing upward every few seconds. On the second-class promenade, she noticed a boy standing alone, his back to the railing. When he turned, she recognized him. His face was pale and strained like it had been up on the boat deck.

Laughter from above drew Karolina's attention. She saw a girl with windblown auburn hair, her stylish skirts fluttering in the breeze. Was she the heiress? Karolina stared. The girl was only a few years older than she was. Karolina tried to imagine having more than seven thousand dollars every year to spend as she chose. After a few seconds, she shook her head. She couldn't imagine having that much money. Her father had always said that great wealth was usually a great evil. He had spent his life helping the poor, ministering to the sick. Now he was gone. Karolina looked at the elegant people. Why were all of them alive when her parents were not?

CHAPTER THREE

Gavin tried to work faster. He had over a hundred pounds of carrots to run through the chopping machines before he could quit for the night. He was looking forward to watching his friends play poker. He looked forward to anything that took his mind off the endless ocean surrounding the *Titanic*.

He had been up on deck that morning again, but it wasn't getting any better. The thought of the Atlantic stretching in every direction made him nearly sick with fear. And now there was the constant lookout for icebergs. Lionel said that even if they struck one, the *Titanic* had been designed so well it couldn't possibly sink. But all

the talk of icebergs made Gavin nervous anyway. He spent his nighttime hours up on deck;
he could barely stand his airless little cabin up in
the bow—especially once his three roommates
were settled in for the night. Wallace snored.
Harry talked in his sleep—sometimes he recited
recipes he was memorizing. Lionel was mad-
deningly tolerant of everyone else's foibles.

"Are you daydreaming, Reilly?" Startled,
Gavin looked up. Harry was grinning at him. "I
sure wish you would play poker tonight, Gavin.
As asleep as you are, I'd win all your money."

Gavin shrugged. "All you think about is
money, Harry."

"A man can't afford to pass up opportunity,
Gavin." Harry grinned again, then walked away.
Gavin bent back over the carrots, concentrating
on getting them clean. The vegetable cook was
very particular.

When his shift finally ended, Gavin eased
open one of the heavy double doors and slipped
into the cavernous first-class dining room. At first
glance, it appeared empty. Any of the wealthy
passengers who wanted food now would have to

go to the Parisian Café or the À la Carte Restaurant up on C-deck.

The decorative pillars and arches that divided the huge room looked eerie in the dim light. On the far side, Gavin spotted Wallace and Harry. They had turned up the table lamp. Harry's white shirtsleeves were pushed up over his skinny arms. Heavyset Wallace sprawled casually in his chair, his elbows propped on the carved wood of the armrests. His rust-colored hair looked almost orange in the lamplight.

Gavin glanced up at the ornate ceiling. The endless geometric knot pattern scrolled its way among the pillars, making angular shadows on the white surface.

"Come on, Gavin, let's play a hand before the others get here," Wallace called.

Gavin started across the plush carpet, making his way between the tables. The snowy linen napkins were folded into careful twin peaks, the silverware polished and laid out precisely on the white tablecloths. He was careful not to disturb anything.

Harry grinned as Gavin got closer. "There's no point trying to talk him into this, and you know it, Wallace."

Gavin shrugged. "You both know why I can't."

"He thinks he's going to be the next John Jacob Astor," Wallace sneered. In the lamplight his freckles were hard to see.

Gavin smiled. "All I want is steady work and a better life."

Wallace shook his head. "You think too small, Gavin. Do you think the Americans will greet you with open arms at the dock?"

"Leave him alone, Wallace," Harry put in.

"Nothing wrong with ambition, is there, Harry?" Wallace argued. "Not everyone wants to rule the galley. Some of us want to rule the world."

Harry nodded wisely and shuffled the cards. "Not me. Better to have a dream you can reach. I want to become a chef and I want to see the world."

"You're going to end up seeing very little beyond pots and chopping machines," Wallace growled.

"Harry has a bright future with the White Star Line, Wallace." They all turned to see Lionel walking toward them, stepping sideways to pass between the tables. Gavin watched him approach. Lionel's chiseled features and elegant manners made him seem at home in this grand room. He took off his steward's jacket and hung it carefully over the back of a chair, then sat down. "Pull up a chair, Gavin. You can watch me win all of Wallace's money again."

Wallace grimaced. "I'm feeling lucky tonight, Lionel."

Gavin pulled in a deep breath. "I think I'll go up to the boat deck instead."

"What do you do up there, anyway?" Harry asked, shuffling the cards.

Gavin looked aside, trying to think of something to tell them. He wasn't about to tell them how cooped up he felt—or how afraid he was to go on deck during the day. "I've been in that hot galley since I got up this morning. I want to see the stars."

Lionel yawned and stretched, leaning back in his chair. He took off his bow tie and tucked it into his jacket pocket. "You grew up on a farm, didn't you?"

Gavin nodded. "You know I did."

"We all know, Gavin," Wallace said, laughing. "You still have cow dung on your shoes and a kitchen chair haircut. You know, you should go down to C-deck and see the barber once in a while."

Gavin glared at him. Wallace loved to make other people feel small. Lionel was shaking his head. "You will never get farther than the scullery, Wallace. You have no manners at all."

Wallace frowned. "You think you belong in first class because you work there. Next thing we know, you'll be exercising in the squash court and expecting to be allowed in the swimming bath."

"Lionel earned his position," Gavin said.

Harry looked up. "You're just envious, Wallace."

Gavin grinned. "I'll stay for a while, just to listen to you insult each other." He slid a chair back. His roommates laughed.

"I saw an iceberg bigger than a barn today," Lionel said.

The laughter died down.

"I've seen growlers all along—" Wallace began.

"No," Lionel interrupted. "Not a growler, a big one."

As Harry shuffled the deck and began to deal the cards, Gavin glanced out the windows at the darkness, involuntarily clenching his hands into fists.

"This is the *Titanic*, Gavin," Harry said. "You don't need to go silent and scared on us."

"That's what he's good at," Wallace jeered. "You ever see him up on the boat deck all pale and sweaty?"

Before Gavin could answer, Lionel leaned forward. "Leave Gavin alone, Wallace. Any ship can sink. Even this one."

Tired of the insults, Gavin shoved back his chair. "If I'm going to get any fresh air tonight, I'd better get going now."

"All that talk about icebergs got to you, didn't it, Gavin?" Wallace taunted him.

Gavin waved without answering and walked back across the dining saloon. His stomach was churning, and all he could think about was how much he needed to be outside, to breathe clean, cold air. Thank God it was nighttime.

Just to see, Karolina crossed to the locked door and tried the handle. It wouldn't budge. Not surprised, she turned and hurried up the narrow corridor, buttoning her coat and feeling guilty. Aunt Rose had gone to bed early, and Karolina knew that if she woke up, she'd be worried. But there just wasn't any other choice. The tiny stateroom allowed Karolina no privacy, and she felt the pressing ache behind her eyes that meant she needed time to cry. She knew only one place on the whole ship where she might be able to be completely alone.

Most of the third-class stateroom doors were wide open. People stood talking in the doorways, their voices hushed. It was hot, and the air was thick with human noise and odors. It felt good to be walking—to be anywhere except in their little stateroom.

Emily and her children had come to visit for part of the day. Emily was sweet-natured and fun to talk to, but Davey was cranky. Karolina understood him perfectly. It was awful to be shut up all day long in the tiny third-class cabins.

The entrance to the stairway was crowded, but most of the people there were just standing in small groups, talking quietly. Karolina excused herself, making her way through them until she could start upward.

She'd been all the way up to the boat deck twice; she never got tired of the sea wind or the slate-gray water. She had once managed to slip onto the first-class promenade, but had been afraid to go more than a little ways along it. She knew her cotton dress and plain coat marked her as very different from the first-class passengers.

The stairs were pretty steep, but Karolina went up at a quick, even pace. When she passed the third-class general room, three older men were coming out. They were deep in discussion, speaking their own language. None of them glanced her way as she turned toward the promenade.

The starry sky was clear, and Karolina stood

for a few moments, pulling in deep breaths of clean air. Then she started off again. The cargo hoists looked like ghostly giant birds as she passed between them and opened the door that led to the second-class stairs.

As she had been the first time, she was amazed at the difference between steerage class and second class. Here, the walls were covered with beautifully grained oak. The balustrade was ornate, and the carpet beneath her feet was soft.

There were fewer people here, too, but she looked straight ahead at the patterned carpet to avoid meeting anyone's eyes as she started upward. Third-class passengers were expected to stay below. She was certain that any steward who saw her would ask where her cabin was, then insist that she go back down to steerage.

"Come on, John, let's go see what it's like."

Karolina looked up at the sound of the girl's voice. She was fair skinned, her lustrous hair pulled back in a pink ribbon that matched her dress. She was leaning on the oak balustrade, frowning, her eyes narrowed. Karolina looked away.

"Come on."

From the corner of her eye, Karolina saw the girl stamp her foot petulantly.

"I'm going back up," a boy's voice answered from above. "Father said we were to be in the stateroom at ten, and I want to go see the gymnasium, not a crowd of unwashed immigrants." As he finished, he came around the corner and started down the stairs toward Karolina. He was younger than the girl, but he had the same proud, haughty manner.

Pretending to be lost in thought, Karolina veered toward him, bumping into him so hard that he nearly lost his balance. "I'm so sorry," she murmured as she went past. He cursed at her, but she didn't look back at him. Instead, she climbed even faster, crossing the B-deck landing almost at a run. Every other time she had come this way, she had stopped to look at the paintings with their dramatic frames and their muted scenes of forests. This time, she just wanted to get away from everyone.

She emerged onto A-deck, turning to follow the last flight of stairs upward between the two halves of the Palm Court. She stopped to catch her breath, looking into the arched windows. It was so beautiful inside.

Ivy grew on trellises set against the walls. The white wicker furniture was arranged neatly around both oval and square tables. In the back, a party of ten or twelve people laughed aloud, sharing some joke.

Karolina slid past the windows, starting up the last flight of stairs. She was still breathing hard, using one hand to pull herself upward. The polished oak banister felt smooth and cool beneath her hand.

As she pushed open the heavy doors, she shivered in the sudden chill of the cold air and pulled her coat tightly around herself, scanning the deck. She had been right. This was perfect. It was so chilly, no one else was there. Tightening her collar, she walked to the railing. For the first time all day, she allowed herself to think about her mother and father. The ache behind her eyes spilled over, and she felt tears on her cheeks.

"Are you lost? What are you doing up here this late?"

Karolina whirled around. It was the boy she had talked to before. Was he a steward? Most of them were English, and she was pretty sure his accent was Irish. It was too dark to see the expression on his face.

"I'm not lost, thank you." Karolina half-turned, hoping that he would leave her alone.

"My name is Gavin Reilly," he said. "I work in the first- and second-class galley. I don't care if you're up here after lights out."

Karolina stared at him again. "I'm Karolina Truman," she said cautiously, then turned back to face the water.

"Steward?"

Karolina recognized the demanding voice instantly. It was the boy she had encountered on the staircase. His sister was right behind him.

"I say, can you help us? Which way is the gymnasium?" Then the boy saw Karolina and pointed. "She's up from steerage."

Karolina stiffened, but Gavin stood up, straightening his shoulders. "The gymnasium is

up that way. Just keep walking and you will
see it."

The girl looked back once, but neither of
them said any more. Once they were out of
earshot, Karolina glared at Gavin. "I'm not
hurting anything. I just wanted to be alone."

"I hate it below decks," he told her, and
Karolina heard the absolute sincerity in his
voice. "But I can't stand to look at the open
water. It's the oddest thing. At home we have a
pond, a big one. I'm a strong swimmer. I can't
figure out why the ocean scares me so bad. I
have to come up here at night."

"That's awful. It's so beautiful," Karolina said.

"I wish I felt that way," Gavin said unhappily.
"But it won't matter when I get to New York. I
can't wait to get off this ship."

"I can," Karolina said quietly. "I wish there
was somewhere I wanted to go." She explained
quickly, telling him why she was going back to
America now. "And I will end up living with
my aunts," she told him. "Rose has never married, and Iris is a widow now. I love them,
but. . . . " Karolina hesitated. She wasn't sure

why she didn't want to live with her aunts. There wasn't anywhere else she wanted to be.

Gavin shook his head. "I'm sorry. It's a hard thing to lose your parents. My da died a year ago."

Karolina ducked her head, her cheeks flaming with embarrassment. What was she doing telling a perfect stranger about her troubles? She could barely talk to Aunt Rose about her parents. Tears filled her eyes. She leaned forward, looking down at the *Titanic*'s lights reflected in the ocean. Then she whirled and walked away from him before he could say anything more.

CHAPTER FOUR

Gavin opened his eyes. "It's time to get up," he said as he did every morning.

"Are you sure?" Wallace demanded from his upper berth.

"He hasn't been more than two minutes off yet," Lionel said.

Gavin heard the tiny chiming of Lionel's pocket watch as it began to strike the hour.

"All we ever do is work," Wallace complained.

"Did you expect to get paid for a pleasure cruise?" Harry teased, and Wallace cursed under his breath.

Gavin rolled out of bed. It was easiest to dress while the others were still in their berths.

Once everyone was up, the small stateroom seemed impossibly cramped.

The ship was rolling gently, and Gavin could feel an irregular rising and falling of the bow as he buttoned his shirt. As always, he fought to keep himself from thinking about the dark water outside the hull. Lionel slid out of bed and reached to turn on the lamp.

Wallace jerked his blanket higher. "Criminy, Lionel, that's too bright!"

Lionel and Gavin exchanged a smile. Wallace was invariably grumpy in the mornings. Harry began to whistle softly as he sat up, then slid down from his upper berth. Gavin combed his hair quickly, without bothering to look in the mirror. A few seconds later he was opening the door.

"See you in the galley," Harry sang out. "I'll be helping the pastry chefs again today."

"You make it sound like a picnic," Wallace grumbled.

"And you make it sound like a day in Hades," Lionel quipped, and they all laughed.

The bow rose, then fell again as Gavin

stepped into the corridor. His stomach churned. He started down the passageway. Without meaning to, he glanced back toward the bow. How much steel was between him and the icy black water? He shook his head, angry with himself.

It was five minutes past four when Gavin got to the galley. The bakers were finishing up as the butchers and pastry cooks got started. Gavin decided to work as fast as he could. If he finished early, maybe he would be able to go up to the second-class library and spend a few hours reading. It sounded like heaven. When he was reading, he couldn't think about the water.

Harry called out a greeting as he came in, and Gavin grinned back at him. Wallace was just behind, slouching along, his morning frown still in place. He would cheer up later, Gavin knew. He had won in the poker game the night before.

Gavin's first job was dicing carrots for the noon meal. He made quick work of washing and chopping them. He carried the diced carrots up to the vegetable cook's table, then rinsed the orange fiber out of the chopping machine.

"Lionel tell you about Wallace winning last night?"

Gavin looked up to see Harry's wry smile. "It was pretty bad, I guess."

Harry nodded. "You're the smart one, I think, keeping your money in your pocket."

"Hurry up with the vegetable marrow, Gavin!"

The sharp tone in the head cook's voice let Gavin know he had been seen talking instead of working. Harry smiled apologetically and bustled away. Gavin turned to one of the pantrymen. "Bring me the parsnips, please."

Gavin crossed the galley, slowing to let men with laden trays and heavy mixing bowls pass ahead of him.

"I need the forcemeat now," he told the assistant butcher.

The tall man nodded briskly. "Give me just a minute to finish up these filets mignons, Gavin."

Walking back through the organized pandemonium, Gavin met the pantryman at his wash basin. Together, they dumped in fifty pounds of parsnips. Gavin picked up his wire brush. He tried hard not to think about anything as he worked. One by one the parsnips lost their coating of dirt and shone milky white under the electric lights.

When the butcher brought him the force-meat, Gavin stirred it into the mashed parsnips, then delivered the mixture to the vegetable cook. Breakfast was served and cleaned up after, then lunch. The hours seemed to drag as Gavin tackled one chore after another.

Midday, Gavin heard shouting. The roast cook was furious. The dinner lamb had been cut thicker than he'd anticipated. For a while, it looked as though it would not be done in time to serve with the salmon, roast duckling, sirloin of beef, and other entrées for the first-class dining room.

Preparing the second-class dinner went much more smoothly, but then it was a simpler meal. There were only four entrées, counting the baked haddock with sharp sauce.

By the time Gavin had cleaned his equipment

and scoured his washbasin that night, it was almost ten o'clock. Working fast hadn't made any difference at all. If anything, he was more tired than usual. But he still wanted to go up to the boat deck. He needed to get out, at least for a little while.

Gavin thought about taking the lift up to A-deck, but it was forbidden. He would be conspicuous standing next to the first-class passengers in their expensive, formal clothing. He started up the long staircase, hoping that by the time he had gone up and climbed back down, he would be tired enough to fall asleep.

"Do you know what Emily told me today?" Aunt Rose was saying as she got ready for bed.

Karolina tried to look interested. "What?"

"That couple two cabins down—the ones with five children—Emily says she's pregnant again. Can you imagine?"

Karolina shook her head. "I'm going to go for a little walk."

Aunt Rose settled her nightgown across her shoulders and turned to face Karolina. "They turned off the lights twenty minutes ago. It's well after ten."

Karolina shrugged. "I can't stand being cooped up down here. Besides, they don't turn off the lights in first- or second-class until later."

"Maybe you should wait until tomorrow." Aunt Rose reached up and began unpinning her hair. "We won't be cooped up much longer. In two days we'll be back in New York."

Karolina nodded again, but she glanced toward the door.

"Oh, go on, then," Aunt Rose said. "But don't stay on deck long. Emily said it's much colder this evening. I would go with you, but you know how hard the stairs are for me."

Karolina barely heard the last sentence. She was reaching for her coat and backing out the door. Once she was out in the narrow corridor, she turned and started walking—fast. She could hear the muted sound of people singing a hymn as she negotiated the narrow hall. She recognized it: "Now the Day Is Ended." It had been one of her father's favorites.

Karolina stopped to press her ear against the wall. Tears filled her eyes as she listened to the people on the other side. The hymn ended, and she could hear a man speaking. Even though she couldn't quite make out his words, it was apparent from the rise and fall of his voice that he was preaching. Transfixed by memories of her father, Karolina allowed herself to cry. No one came down the corridor until she had dried her eyes, and she was grateful. She pulled her coat tighter and headed for the boat deck.

The stairways seemed even longer than usual. There was a big crowd inside the second-class smoking room, and Karolina could hear the men talking and laughing as she hurried past. By the time she finally came out into the still cold air, she was breathing hard. She looked toward the bow, then stepped out onto the boat deck.

"Karolina?"

Startled, she turned toward the sound of Gavin's voice. He was sitting on one of the high-backed benches. She found herself smiling, glad to see him.

"If you came up here to be alone again, I'll find another bench," Gavin said.

"I don't know why I came up here tonight," Karolina said honestly. "I just started feeling like I was going to explode."

Gavin nodded so gravely that she wondered if he really did understand. "Do you want to walk?" he asked her. "I mean, if you don't prefer being alone."

Karolina hesitated, then nodded. "I would like to walk. I've been too afraid of the stewards to really look around up here."

Gavin stood up and waited for her to start off. Then he fell in beside her. Karolina kept glancing at him as they went, sure that he would tell her they couldn't go very far. But he just kept walking past a row of arched windows.

Inside them, Karolina could see opulent leather couches and chairs. The woodwork was ornate. There were small tables around the perimeter, and a long table was set in the center of the room. There was a fireplace with a painting hung above it. Here and there men sat talking, smoking their pipes and cigars. A waiter carried a tray filled with heavy goblets of an amber liquor.

"Let's cross to port side," Gavin said.

Karolina nodded, eager to keep going. They passed a glowing grid, and she stared at it.

"That's the first-class stairway. Have you seen it?" Karolina shook her head. "You should see the Grand Staircase. This one is beautiful, but that one. . . . " He shook his head.

"Reilly! I thought I might find you up here."

Walking toward them was a tall, light-haired young man. He wore a steward's uniform. Karolina glanced at Gavin, sure they were about to get into trouble. Gavin stopped, and she stood beside him. "Karolina Truman, this is my friend Lionel."

Karolina blushed with relief and embarrassment as the young man half-bowed and introduced himself.

Gavin told him that Karolina had never seen the Grand Staircase. "Do you think we could manage that, Lionel?"

"I think we can," he said, looking at Gavin,

then meeting Karolina's eyes. "I bet we can get a glimpse into the gymnasium, too. It's so cold that everyone is staying in tonight."

"I would be most grateful," Karolina said, feeling lighter and freer than she had in a long time.

"It must be close to eleven now. The concerts are over, aren't they?" Gavin said.

"Yes, both landings are clear. The musicians have packed up and gone to bed," Lionel said.

"Let's get going, then," Gavin said. "Port side is easier—we can walk straight through."

Karolina followed him, noticing his nervous glances at the water. It was unnerving tonight, she thought. The sea was absolutely black, but the sky was so clear that the stars sparkled in a smooth curve all the way to the horizon.

"It's colder than last night," Gavin said, pulling the collar of his jacket higher around his neck.

"It is," Lionel agreed. "But we'll be back inside soon enough."

Two women passed, dressed in white furs. One of them had piled her hair so high on her head it bobbed a little with every step she took. They turned and headed for the glowing grid that covered the first-class stairway. Karolina heard them laughing quietly as they pulled open the heavy door.

Gavin had dropped back a half step, letting Lionel go first. Karolina walked fast to keep up with them, acutely conscious of her worn coat and scuffed shoes. They passed through yellow pools of light that poured through the high, arched windows. The lamps seemed almost too bright against the ink-dark backdrop of the moonless night.

Karolina was shivering by the time Lionel opened the door and motioned for them to wait. After a few seconds he was back, gesturing at them to come in. Karolina stepped through the door quickly, then stopped and caught her breath.

"Isn't it something?" Gavin said from behind her.

Karolina could only nod. It was incredible. There were two sets of stairs. Each curved gracefully downward to a landing where they joined. From there, a gilt-brightened balustrade ran down the center of the widened staircase as it descended even farther. Above the landing was an intricate carving of two robed women, their faces and hair detailed, almost lifelike. Between them was an ornate clock. It was eleven-thirty.

Karolina tried to soak in the loveliness of the deep-grained wood, the elaborate carvings. She timidly touched the intricate ironwork and gilding that decorated the balustrades. "It's like a fairy tale."

Gavin smiled and gestured, pointing straight up.

Karolina lifted her head and nearly gasped aloud. Above them was a glass dome, supported by arching ironwork.

"It's even prettier in the daylight with the sun shining through it," Lionel said.

Karolina stared at the exquisite dome, tilting her head back so far that her neck began to ache. When she looked back down, both Gavin and Lionel were smiling at her. She blushed again. "I must seem an utter idiot to you both."

"I stood here for half an hour the first time I saw it," Gavin said, and she was grateful for his kindness.

"Let's see the gymnasium before someone sees us," Lionel said. "Officers' quarters are just fore of where we are standing now."

"I don't want to cause trouble or—"

"If anyone asks, we can just say you were lost and we're showing you the way back," Lionel interrupted. Gavin nodded, agreeing with him.

Karolina followed them across the landing. Lionel opened a door, and they all went through. The gymnasium was a long, well-lit room with tall, arching windows that looked out onto the boat deck. It was empty, except for odd-looking machines installed in neat rows on the floor.

"That's the mechanical camel," Lionel explained. "There was a woman riding it for at least an hour yesterday. That low one is a row-ing machine—and on that side's a stationary bicycle."

Karolina looked at the equipment, aston-ished. Her father would have thought all this an incredible extravagance. People who worked for a living got all the exercise anyone could want.

"I know what you are thinking," Gavin said, smiling at her. "We all think the same thing. But many of these people have maids and butlers and cooks. They never lift a finger unless they want to."

"I'd like to be that well off," Lionel laughed. "Don't tell me you don't have the same ambition, Gavin. I won't believe you if you do."

Karolina listened to them bantering. Her father had always insisted on a simple life. Had her mother ever dreamed of wearing furs and bright gems? Karolina felt the familiar sad heaviness seeping back into her heart. She bit at her lower lip. Aunt Rose would start to worry before too much longer.

"Are you all right?" Gavin asked, looking into her face.

She nodded. "I should probably get back now. This is lovely. Thank you both so much." She blinked, hoping neither of them would notice that her eyes had filled with tears.

Lionel gestured toward a door on the far side of the gymnasium. Following him, Karolina dug her fingernails into her palms until the urge to cry subsided. When Gavin held the door open, she stepped into the dark night, relishing the sting of the cold air on her cheeks.

Lionel said good night and left them, walking toward the bow.

"I can walk you back," Gavin offered.

"Don't you want to go below?" Karolina asked.

"I'm all right at night now," he said. "If I don't think about it."

Karolina began to walk, staying close to the arching windows of the gymnasium so that Gavin wouldn't have to come too close to the rail and the black ocean beyond it. She glanced at him, then out at the water. "Oh, my God," she breathed. "Oh, my dear God!"

CHAPTER FIVE

Gavin turned when he heard the fear in Karolina's voice. Looming above the ship's rail, so close that it seemed he could reach out and touch it, was a jagged mass of ice. An iceberg? This close? He spun on his heel, looking instinctively toward the bridge. Hadn't Captain Smith seen it?

At that instant, there was a shuddering of the deck beneath his feet, a movement so subtle, it was easy to wonder whether the deck had trembled or if his own legs were shaking. Chunks of ice tumbled onto the deck, sliding, skittering across the smooth surface, smashing into the funnel housing.

There was an odd scraping sound above the

usual noise of the engines. Gavin held still, his breath coming fast. Even if they had hit the iceberg, the *Titanic* would be all right, wouldn't it?

"What was that?" Karolina whispered. "Did you feel that?"

Gavin didn't answer. He heard shouts from somewhere up by the bridge. He tried to spot Lionel. Lionel would know what was happening—if there was anything to worry about. The mass of ice was sliding past now, angling off to one side. Gavin realized suddenly that the night had become too silent. The huge engines had stopped. A second after he thought it, the silence exploded into a hissing roar.

Gavin flinched, his teeth chattering. He turned in a full circle. He was pretty sure that the noise wasn't dangerous. It meant that the engineers had closed down the steam valves, that was all. It was the fastest way to stop the ship.

He explained the noise as well as he could to Karolina, yelling close to her ear. "You should go back down. It's all right," he finished, straightening up to look into her face.

She was pale, staring at him. "But we hit the iceberg!"

Gavin tried to think. "There are waterproof compartments in the hull," he shouted over the roaring of the excess steam. "It won't sink." He watched Karolina take a deep breath.

Gavin's heart was thudding inside his chest as he looked out over the water. It was so dark, so cold. And it was miles deep. Karolina shivered violently, and Gavin gripped her shoulder. "Go back to your stateroom and keep your life belt close, just in case." He waited until she nodded, but she didn't move. He leaned close to her ear. "I'll come get you if there's any real danger."

Karolina stared into his eyes for a second. Then she nodded again. "Third-class. Number fifty-five. Promise?" Her voice cracked, but he could understand her.

"I promise," he said, nodding. She whirled and was gone.

Gavin watched her run, then turned toward the bow. Unbelievably, there were a few men *playing* with the ice. Gavin stared as they kicked it back and forth. Abruptly, the roaring lessened.

Gavin could hear voices; a man and a woman were arguing somewhere nearby. He couldn't understand any of their words, only the sharp, strained tone of their voices. He began to walk. If anyone knew anything, it would be the officers on the bridge. They would never let him up there, he was sure, but maybe he could overhear something—or maybe there would be someone coming off the bridge he could ask.

"Hey, you! Steward?"

Gavin spun around, startled. A woman was walking toward him. She had a dressing gown wrapped tightly around her. "Are we safe?" she demanded in a shrill, loud voice. "My mother sent me up to find out. She's the kind to worry over every little thing. I told her that nothing could be very wrong. Is it?"

Gavin stared at her, trying to make sense out of her rush of words. He was unable to say anything at all for a few seconds. "I don't know," he finally managed. "I'm not a steward. I'm sorry."

The woman's face was twisted with annoyance. She turned on her heel and strode away. Gavin squinted in the darkness. Ahead of him, where the lights shone along the side of the bridge, he could see a group of dark-jacketed stewards. They were talking, gesturing, obviously agitated. Gavin felt a tremor of fear. It looked like they were arguing.

". . . sound a general alarm," one voice rose above the others.

"That's up to Captain Smith," someone answered.

Gavin slowed his step, straining to hear more, but the jumble of voices stopped suddenly as a door opened and an officer came onto the bridge, bellowing orders.

"Get the passengers into their life belts!" Then he turned and spoke to someone on the bridge Gavin couldn't see. "Get the lifeboats uncovered."

The stewards started off in every direction as the officer went back inside. Gavin stood staring. Lifeboats. That meant they thought the *Titanic* was going to sink. Would the passengers even know how to get up to the lifeboats? At dinner, he had heard Wallace talking about Captain Smith's refusal to run a lifeboat practice

that morning during the emergency drill—
even though the White Star Line was known
for its Sunday morning lifeboat drills.

"Gavin?" The familiar voice startled him
into turning around. Lionel was speaking
loudly enough to be heard over the dull roar of
the escaping steam. "Listen to me. Go get your
life belt."

Gavin nodded, wishing he could be as calm
as Lionel seemed to be. Thoughts of the deep
black water tugged at him, and he tried to push
them out of his mind. Suddenly, the roaring of
the steam intensified into a screaming hiss
again. It drowned out whatever else Lionel was
trying to say. Lionel pushed at him, pointing
emphatically toward the bow. Then he wheeled
around and ran toward the first-class entrance.

Glancing at the men who were still playing
their mock game of football with the fallen ice,
Gavin made his way forward, past the bridge.
He descended the steps that led down to the
well deck and opened the door to a narrow ser-
vice stairway. It was empty, but once the door
closed behind him, and the roaring of the steam

was muted, he heard an odd, resonating mur-mur.

Clumsy with panic, he still tried to hurry. He timed his steps quickly, the way he and Lionel often did, nearly flying down the metal stairs. The murmuring got louder as he passed the C-deck landing and continued downward. Voices, he realized; it was the sound of frightened voices.

As he passed the D-deck landing, he could see people milling in the corridor and he could hear more clearly, but it made no differ-ence. Many of them were speaking languages he didn't understand.

Without warning, an old man lunged at Gavin. His wrinkled face was shadowed with fear. He held Gavin's forearm tightly with one hand, talking earnestly, repeating the same few words over and over.

Gavin shook his head. "I can't understand you. I'm sorry." He struggled to get away as the man made a wide, paddling gesture with his free hand, all the while shaking his head vio-lently from side to side. It suddenly made sense to Gavin—the man was explaining that he could not swim.

Gavin shook his head helplessly, trying to step away. He finally managed to break free and bolted, afraid the man would grab him again. Angry shouts followed Gavin as he started downward once more.

Where the stairs opened onto E-deck, Gavin leaped off the landing, running down a passage he knew would take him through the third-class cabins to the crew's quarters—foremost in the bow.

Here, the passageway was crowded, and Gavin had to make his way through frightened people—as well as stacks of clothing and trunks that nearly filled the corridor. The men were mostly silent, their faces tense and worried. Mothers were holding their children tightly, bundles of belongings clutched beneath their arms.

Where the crowds thinned, Gavin sprinted, sliding around corners, his own thoughts a fearful tangle. Without slowing his pace he turned to the left, heading for the next set of stairs. He started downward. He had to get his wallet and he wanted the picture of his family. Beyond that, he had only two sets of clothes and he could wear them in layers to keep out the freezing air. Or was it foolish to take the time to dress?

Gripping the handrail, he neared the bottom of the stairs and tensed himself to leap again. Midmotion, just as he was leaning forward to jump, he saw, for the first time, the landing below him. It was flooded with water.

CHAPTER SIX

Karolina was still running. Down here, the roaring was distant, not even loud enough to waken someone from sleep. The stairways and the corridors were empty, all the cabin doors closed for the night. The sound of her own footsteps seemed rude, out of place, in the peaceful midnight silence.

Her stateroom door was shut tight. Aunt Rose had not awakened. Karolina turned the handle and went in. The stuffy little room was quiet except for Aunt Rose's gentle snoring. Karolina was about to shake her aunt awake. Then she paused. What if it was all a false alarm?

Karolina stood breathing deeply in the darkness, still unsure what to do. She stepped back and knelt down, feeling for their life belts beneath her berth. It took a moment for her to find them. "Aunt Rose," Karolina said quietly. There was no response. "Please wake up." Her aunt turned beneath the blankets, sighing. Karolina reached out to touch her shoulder.

"What?" Aunt Rose said thickly. "What's the matter?" Karolina turned on the light. Aunt Rose sat up, blinking. "Whatever in the world is the matter?"

"We have to put these on now." Karolina held out the life belts.

"What are you talking about?" Aunt Rose sat up straighter, pulling the blanket along with her. "Where have you been, young lady? I waited for a long time. I must have dozed, but I—"

"We're supposed to put on our life belts," Karolina said once more. She knew she should explain, but it was hard, here in the bright light, looking at her aunt's irritated face. "There was an iceberg," she began. Aunt Rose's expression changed, and Karolina began telling her about Gavin—and the iceberg. When she finished, Aunt Rose frowned.

"I didn't feel anything. If we hit it, then shouldn't I have felt something?"

"I did," Karolina said. Then she hesitated. "There was a scraping sound, then the engines went off, and there was steam pouring out of the funnels instead of smoke. It made an awful sound."

Aunt Rose shook her head. "I'm sure they'll tell us if anything is really wrong."

Karolina held out one of the life belts again. "Gavin said to put these on. I think we ought to."

Aunt Rose took the belt, but set it down on the bed beside her. "And what does this Gavin do? He works in the galley?"

Karolina pulled the bulky life belt over her head. The cloth-covered floats were stiff and uncomfortable. "I want to go up on deck and find out—"

Aunt Rose shook her head, interrupting. "If your mother knew I had let you go out cavorting with a young man, she would turn over in her grave. I had no idea that you were doing such things, Karolina."

Karolina fumbled with the straps on her life

belt. "You don't understand, Aunt Rose—"

"I understand perfectly, young lady. I have been entirely too lax with you. I thought you just were strolling around, or that you would fall into proper company with other girls."

"I didn't do anything wrong. And I got to see the Grand Staircase. It's so beautiful—"

"Karolina, it's the middle of the night. Get to bed."

"I *saw* the iceberg, Aunt Rose."

"They told us any emergency would sound the alarms, Karolina. Perhaps this boy Gavin was playing a joke on you?"

Karolina pulled in a deep breath. "He wouldn't do that." She paused. "Aunt Rose, we should at least ask someone. Gavin thought everything was going to be all right and he said he'd come tell us if it wasn't, but—"

Aunt Rose nodded knowingly. "And he is probably with his friends now, having a good laugh at a gullible girl."

Karolina dropped onto her berth. Maybe Aunt Rose was partly right. If they had hit the iceberg hard enough to cause any damage, surely there would have been more than that vague little tremor she had felt. And she hadn't heard any commotion at all. The iceberg probably had given everyone a start, then just floated past. But why couldn't she feel the usual vibration from the engines?

"If you have a grain of sense, you'll sleep now," Aunt Rose said. "I don't want you going up there anymore." Without another word, she slid beneath her blankets and rolled over.

Karolina stood up and turned off the light. Then she sat on the edge of her berth again, listening. There were a few voices outside the door. Karolina heard a woman talking quietly, calmly. No alarms sounded. After a time, the voices faded.

Aunt Rose was probably right. There was no commotion, no disturbance. After a few minutes, Karolina pulled her life belt off, then her coat. Without undressing, she lay down, resting her head uneasily on her pillow.

"Oh, God," Gavin breathed. "Oh, sweet Jesus, no." He stared at the water at the foot of the stairs. Where was it coming from? The little bump, the scraping sound—how badly had the hull been punctured?

"Leave it," a man yelled from farther down the corridor.

"We can't," a woman's voice objected.

Gavin couldn't hear the man's answer. Someone else was shouting in what sounded like Italian. A woman screamed, and a baby cried. Shaking, Gavin stepped into the water, starting toward his cabin.

Here on F-deck, the corridors were choked with desperate people. Gavin made his way over piles of wet clothes, soaked cases, and bags. He apologized to men and women who stared at him without really seeing him.

Gavin's cabin door was shut. He shoved it open, sending up a little spray of water. Wallace's trunk was open. He had been here and gone. Harry often stayed late in the galley, watching the pastry cooks start the next day's croissants or piecrusts.

"Are we going to die?"

Gavin spun around to see a boy of about eight or nine peering into the open door. He carried a bundle of books under one arm. His face was so eager, so frightened, that Gavin forced himself to smile. "Of course not. Didn't anyone tell you about the *Titanic*?"

The boy nodded. "My da says she's the biggest ship ever built."

"And the safest," Gavin told him, wondering how big a lie he was telling. "Where's your family?"

The boy pointed down the corridor. "Mum is packing up."

"Tell her to hurry," Gavin said. "That way, if we have to change ships, you can be near the head of the line. Tell her a steward told you that," Gavin finished.

The boy nodded once, then disappeared. The instant he had gone, Gavin jerked open his own trunk. He dug through the clothes, pulling on his sweater. He lifted out his second-best shoes, carefully setting them on the berth to keep dry as he grabbed his wallet and the small photograph of his family from the trunk. He stuffed a clean pair of socks into each shoe, then tied them together. He slung them over his shoulder, sliding his wallet into his trousers and the photo into his shirt pocket. Then he turned, the icy water splashing around his feet.

Halfway down the passage, Gavin realized that the water was deeper. It had risen almost to his ankles in the few minutes he had been in his room. He hurried as fast as he could, stepping around people who refused to get out of his way, shouting at everyone to get up to the boat deck as quickly as possible.

A woman with a scarf tied tightly over her hair stood weeping, leaning against the wall. Gavin spoke to her, motioning, trying to get her to understand she had to go upward. She shrugged, answering in a sad voice in a musical language.

Gavin took the woman's hand, pulling her toward the stairs. She came with him, almost without resistance. As she did, she stopped crying. Tears wet her cheeks as she followed him, sloshing through the cold, deepening water.

Gavin led her through the crowd, wishing he could ask her if she had family or companions on the ship. The instant the thought came to him, he remembered. If her cabin was here in the bow, it meant she was married. Unmarried people in third class were segregated—men in the bow, women in the stern.

Gavin stopped. "Where's your husband?" he said, slowly and distinctly. The woman tilted her head, obviously puzzled. "Your husband," Gavin repeated. He pointed at a couple making their way past, gesturing at the man. "Husband."

The woman seemed to understand him this time. She said a few words in her own tongue, lifting her hands palms up. She made a trailing, circular gesture, then pointed at the stairs ahead of them. Gavin started off again, the woman close behind him.

It was harder to get through the passages now. More and more people were trying to get themselves and their belongings above decks. The main stairways were a tortuous crush of people.

"Katya!"

The man's voice was so close that Gavin whirled to face him. The woman began talking, a jumble of words. The man clasped Gavin's shoulder, smiling into his face. "*Spaciba. Spaciba!*"

Gavin could only nod as the man guided his wife away, his arm tightly around her shoulders. Then the crowd closed in, and Gavin couldn't see them. A thick odor of wet cloth, sweat, and stale air enclosed him as he fought to make his way upward.

On D-deck, Gavin stumbled aside, breaking free, his spare shoes bouncing against his shoulder as he darted down a corridor that led away from the third-class entrance. He had to get to the third-class cabins in the stern to tell Karolina and her aunt to get up to the boat deck. There was every chance that the captain would decide to move passengers from the *Titanic* to another ship. If there was panic, passengers could easily get trampled on the main stairways—or trapped below decks by the crush of frightened people.

Gavin crossed the third-class open space. The floor was dry here. No one was using the big, unfurnished room now; none of the passengers felt like taking a walk this late at night. Gavin tried to think clearly, mapping a route in his mind. He knew D-deck better than any other since that was where he had spent most of his time aboard the *Titanic*. But there was no way to get to the stern from here unless he went upward. He started up the stairs in the corner of the open room, taking them two at a time.

At the top, he emerged into the freezing night air. He was breathing hard. It took him a moment to realize that the roar of steam from the funnels had stopped. He could hear the band playing somewhere above him. It was a lively tune and it seemed out of place, like music from a dream. He crossed the forward well deck, slowing to a walk, trying to catch his breath. There were officers on the bridge. He could hear them shouting orders.

Gavin went up the steps to C-deck, then, without pausing, headed straight on toward B-deck. There was no other way to get to Karolina's room fast enough.

He pulled open the door to the first-class corridor, expecting to see dozens of people frantically packing their bags and cases. But it was almost empty, and he saw no stacked luggage at all.

Gavin walked so fast, he was almost running. He passed a few people talking quietly as they headed toward the Boat-deck. He kept his face averted, out of habit. Unauthorized intrusion into first class was strictly against the rules.

"Steward?"

Gavin turned to see a man in formal evening attire standing in the doorway of one of the staterooms. Behind him, a woman in a dressing gown looked out anxiously. Gavin could see the orange-red glow of their electric heater behind them. "I'm not a steward, sir," he admitted.

"Do you know what has happened? Our steward brought us these." The man held out two life belts, their stiff cork cores making them awkward for him to hold.

"I think you should put them on, sir," Gavin said carefully. "And then go up to the boat deck."

"But it's so cold," the man's wife said from

behind him. "Do we have to go up there?"

Gavin shrugged. "It would probably be safest, ma'am."

The man dismissed Gavin with a wave, then turned and ushered his wife back inside their room. Gavin could hear them talking as he walked away.

Crossing the broad hallway that brought him to the Grand Staircase, he saw people milling around on the landing. The music was louder here, and he realized the band was just outside.

Gavin started down the beautiful staircase, easily passing through the scattered families and couples who looked almost more excited than frightened. After C-deck, there were more people coming up from below. Walking against the crowd, Gavin stayed near the ornate balustrade, his shoulder brushing the polished paneling.

Here, everyone was remarkably calm. No one carried baggage, but most of the women were dressed in a bulky hodgepodge of expensive clothing. No one was dragging trunks or shouldering bundles of goods here. Some of the women wore mismatched jewelry, no doubt figuring it was safer on them than in their rooms or with the purser.

"Everyone please don your life belts and remain calm," a voice shouted from above. Gavin turned to see an officer in his dark, well-cut uniform. "If you will all just please come up to the boat deck now."

Gavin kept going downward, passing the last of the crowd, finding himself suddenly alone on the stairs. This was what he had been hoping for. He hurried, his footsteps a quick staccato rhythm.

Where the Grand Staircase opened onto the dining saloon reception room, Gavin began to run. He knew exactly where he was going now, and how to get there fast. He shoved open the heavy doors and pounded through the empty first-class dining room. He dodged around the pillars, zigzagging to miss the tables, their snowy linen tablecloths set with silver and glasses for breakfast. The pair of shoes over his shoulder bounced wildly as he ran.

He hit the pantry doors at a run, stiff-arming

them open. There were voices somewhere nearby, but as he rounded the corner, he couldn't see anyone. He ran past the pastry cooks' worktable and sprinted into the galley.

The counters and basins looked as familiar as old friends, and Gavin felt himself calming down a little, slowing his stride to catch his breath. Everything looked normal. Nothing was out of place. The shining steel chopping machines were clean, ready for the next day's work.

"Gavin?" It was Wallace, his round face twisted with fear. He was standing near the back wall. "Gavin, Lionel says she's going to sink."

Gavin's calmness evaporated, leaving behind a dryness in his throat. "Lionel said it?"

Wallace nodded. "I saw him maybe twenty minutes ago. He said he had been up in first class, pounding on people's doors to wake them up. Half of them wouldn't believe him."

"You should get up on the boat deck, Wallace. Where's Harry? Is he with you?"

Wallace shook his head. "I saw him in our stateroom, but he stayed back to help some family carry their baggage, and I haven't seen him since."

Gavin stepped back, turning. "I have to get someone in third class. Then I'll be up there. You just get going."

Wallace pushed off the wall, his eyes focusing on the doors that led back into the pantry. He nodded and slouched his way toward them. Gavin watched him for a second, then started off again at a run. His extra shoes bounced against his shoulder so hard that it hurt. On an impulse he threw them to one side and ran faster. Lionel would never say something like that if he didn't believe it.

The second-class dining saloon was empty except for a few crew members who sat talking quietly on the far side. Gavin recognized two of them, but didn't know their names. The third, a stocky, red-faced man in a steward's uniform, looked up and frowned. Gavin tried to think of his name. Peterson? Or Peters? "There's water pouring into the forward crew cabins," Gavin managed between ragged breaths, staggering to a stop, facing them. "You should all get up to the boat deck now."

The steward shook his head in disapproval. "You'd better not let Captain Smith hear you trying to panic people like that. This is the *Titanic*, boy. She's unsinkable."

CHAPTER SEVEN

Karolina lay for a long time in the darkness, listening to every tiny sound. The engines had not yet started up again, and the silence was unsettling. Her whole body was tense—she was expecting the emergency alarm to go off. But it didn't.

After a few moments, Karolina tried closing her eyes. As the silence went on, she began to calm down. She stretched, willing herself to relax. But she couldn't. Every tiny sound, every creak and whisper of the metal that surrounded her, kept her alert, made her listen harder.

Karolina tried to remember exactly what Gavin had said. He had reassured her, then he had told her that he would come to warn her if anything was really wrong. Karolina pulled in a deep breath and turned onto her side. He had *promised*. A moment later, she flopped back over and stared straight upward into the darkness. What if Gavin couldn't come?

Karolina sat up. It would take only a few minutes for her to run up the stairway and find a steward to ask—or maybe she should just go back up on the boat deck. Without thinking any further, Karolina stood up. She pulled on her coat and crossed the little stateroom.

The door latch made a little clicking sound, but Aunt Rose didn't stir. Karolina eased out into the hallway and closed the door behind her. For an instant she stood still, wondering if she should go back and get her life belt. Then she shook her head. If they were in danger, she would be coming straight back down to get Aunt Rose.

Feeling a prickle of nervousness slide over her skin, Karolina started down the hallway. There were a few people standing in open doorways. In front of the cabins nearest the stairway, two women were dragging a trunk from their room. One was tall and thin. The other was shorter and had long black hair. Karolina stared at them. They would never manage to get the heavy trunk up all those stairs. Unless the gangways were opened—

"Miss? Missy?"

The thin woman was gesturing. Karolina sighed. She pulled her coat tighter around her shoulders. "Yes?"

"My mother cannot walk up all these steps by herself. And I must help my sister with the trunk."

Karolina hesitated. "Have you talked to a steward? Why are you leaving your stateroom?"

The thin woman shrugged. "Because my sister is a crazy."

The dark-haired woman in the doorway made an impatient sound deep in her throat. "I am not crazy. The man said we hit an iceberg head-on and the ship is sinking."

Karolina's legs felt weak. "What man? Who told you that?"

"A drunken man who accosted her in the general room up above." The thin woman pointed upward. "And my sister believed him."

"I saw the iceberg," Karolina said. "I felt a little bump, and there was a scraping sound."

"This is all silly," the thin woman said. "A drunk and a child tell us we hit an iceberg. No one felt anything, there's no alarm, and the steward I asked told me to go back to bed. I'm inclined to believe him." She kicked at the trunk.

"I'm on my way to ask an officer what to do," Karolina told them.

"You should have done that." The thin woman glared at her sister. "You have just about scared Mama to death."

For the first time, Karolina looked past them and saw a frail and elderly lady perched on a trunk. Her eyes were wide, and her posture was rigid.

"I'll be right back down," Karolina offered. "If you're still here, I'll tell you whatever I find out."

"Is that good enough for you?" the thin woman demanded, facing her sister again.

"I don't think we should wait." The dark-haired woman lifted her chin, and the argument began all over again. Karolina turned toward the stairs.

She hurried as fast as she could, slowing only to catch her breath as she topped the C-deck landing. The third-class general room was usually empty by ten when the lights were turned out. Not tonight. Karolina heard voices coming from behind the closed doors. As she came up the last few steps, two men passed her going the other way, their faces grim and worried.

The night was bitterly cold as Karolina stepped out onto the promenade. There was no wind, and still no moon. The awful sound of the steam coming out of the funnels had stopped. What did that mean? There was still no vibration from the engines, either.

Karolina could hear people talking from above and faint strains of music. The band was playing ragtime? At this hour on a Sunday? There was a crowd on the boat deck.

Almost running, Karolina crossed the deck, passing the cargo hoist where little Davey had played. Then she stopped, staring upward at an officer talking to three men on the second-class deck. She went up a few steps, straining to over-hear.

"The Marconi operator has been sending out the CQD since we hit," the officer was say-ing. "It won't be much longer before help arrives."

"Then why risk getting into the lifeboats at all?" one man asked.

The officer smiled. "It's just a precaution, sir."

"I don't like the idea of my wife being swung out over the Atlantic Ocean by a couple of flimsy pulleys." The man shook his head. "Hell, sir. It's sixty feet or more down to the water."

"You have nothing to worry about, sir," the officer said. He was talking loudly, as though he wanted everyone around them to be able to hear. "The Harland and Wolff boys were telling us last night about the Welin davit. It's a new design, made to handle the weight of a full lifeboat. I would trust my wife and family—"

"Karolina Truman!"

Aunt Rose's angry voice startled Karolina, and she turned.

"What in the world. . . ?" Aunt Rose paused to drag in two or three laborious breaths.

Karolina rushed to her side. "Are you all right? You shouldn't have come up the stairs so fast, Aunt Rose. I'm sorry. I just wanted to ask someone if anything—"

"No." Aunt Rose shook her head, still breathing too hard to speak easily. "I can hear the band playing, Karolina," she finished.

"Aunt Rose, I'm not the only one who is worried. Look." Karolina pointed upward at the crowds on the boat deck. Aunt Rose had been about to speak. She hesitated, then closed her mouth.

The sound of a woman crying made them both look upward. The officer was gone. His place by the rail had been taken by a couple. The man was holding his wife close, murmuring a stream of soothing words. Something was odd about their clothing. Their coats seemed awkward, lumpy. Karolina stared, understanding why. She looked at two women standing just behind the couple, then at several men who stood with their back to the rail.

"Look, Aunt Rose. They are all wearing life belts. Come up on the boat deck with me," Karolina pleaded. "I just want to ask someone."

"That seems prudent enough to me," Aunt Rose said, giving in. She started forward, and Karolina took her arm. Together they climbed the stairs. Karolina stopped twice to let Aunt Rose catch her breath.

As they stepped onto B-deck, the second-class entry door swung open. Four beautifully dressed women came out, their fur coats buttoned up to their chins. One of them carried a small dog. Its ears were pricked forward, and it squirmed in her arms. They walked in silence, opening a door that Karolina had never noticed. She got a glimpse of heavy oak furniture. Then the women were gone.

"I'm freezing," Aunt Rose said quietly. "Wish I had a fox coat tonight."

Karolina shivered, then nodded without answering. She led the way again, stepping around a portly couple. "Do you know if we are in danger?" Aunt Rose asked them as they went past.

Karolina turned to hear as the man answered. "I have heard that the ship is going to sink," he said without emotion in his voice.

Karolina saw Aunt Rose go pale. "Oh, my God."

The man smiled confidently. "Don't worry too much. There will be help soon enough. This is a busy shipping lane, and the steward assured us that the distress signals will be honored by any boat that hears them."

"Should we stay up here?" Karolina asked.

The man nodded. "We're going to. Our steward told us it would be wise."

"He also said we should stay near the lifeboats," the man's wife added. "So that we'll be among the first to be ferried to the rescue ship." The man nodded politely and guided his wife on toward the door that led to the stairway.

"That seems sensible," Aunt Rose agreed. "We can just go down and get our things and come right back up, then."

Karolina hesitated. Aunt Rose was still breathing hard. "I could go get our belongings," she said. "By myself."

A scattering of shouts from above made them both look upward. Karolina saw the glaring green trail of a rocket in the ink-black sky. In its garish light, she spotted two small icebergs drifting in the still water. "Do you know the way up to the boat deck, Aunt Rose?" Karolina asked. She could feel her own heartbeat.

"I've never even been up this far," Aunt Rose said. "These stairs are hard for me."

"Lifeboat!" a man shouted above them. "Number seven lifeboat is away!"

"Aunt Rose, we'd better hurry," Karolina said.

"Go on, then," Aunt Rose told her, making a shooing motion with her hands. "Hurry back. I'll stay right here and wait for you. But wake Emily on your way past her cabin. Tell her."

Karolina nodded and took a step back. Another flare shot skyward. She turned and ran, the image of the fiery rocket swimming before her vision.

CHAPTER EIGHT

"You're panicking over nothing," the steward called out as Gavin went through the dining room, veering toward the stairs. Gavin didn't bother to answer him.

At the top, Gavin darted out onto C-deck. The doors to the second-class library had been opened wide. There were people standing inside it, their backs to Gavin. One man was talking in a low voice, and the others were leaning close to listen.

Without slowing, Gavin rounded the corner and dashed out onto the third-class promenade. The shock of the cold night air made him catch his breath. His feet and legs tingled with cold, and he realized for the first time how wet his shoes and trousers had gotten.

Shoving his way into the doors at the top of the third-class entrance, Gavin nearly ran into a bearded man who walked with his arm around a weeping girl. Just behind them, a middle-aged woman with a shrill voice shook her finger at Gavin, speaking in a language he couldn't understand.

At the bottom of the stairs, Gavin looked at the cabin numbers, glancing first to his right. "Fifty-six," he whispered, and started toward that side. Halfway there he could see the next door. It was room sixty-two. He spun around and started back across the landing.

There. Room fifty-five was the first one on the other side. Gavin broke into a run. "Karolina!" he called, knocking. No one answered. He pounded on the door.

"What's all the commotion about?" a woman asked from a cabin across the corridor.

Gavin looked at her. "You should get your things together and get up to the boat deck, ma'am." The woman looked startled, then went back inside.

"Gavin!"

He recognized Karolina's American accent and whirled around to face her. She looked scared. "I'm supposed to meet my aunt up on the boat deck," she said as she came closer. "I'm getting our cases. How bad is it?"

"There's water pouring into the bow," Gavin told her. Saying it aloud made it seem even more real, more terrifying. "The *Titanic* is going to sink." Gavin heard disbelief in his own voice. It was so hard to imagine.

Gavin stepped back as Karolina opened the door and went in. He stared down the passageway. The door to the next stateroom banged open. Two women marched out, dressed warmly. Their faces were prim and composed as they went past without a word.

Karolina came out into the corridor, carrying two leather cases. She had two life belts slung over her shoulder. He took the bigger case. "Is that unlocked?" he asked, pointing at the stairwell door across the corridor.

"It wasn't before," Karolina told him.

He crossed the passageway to try the door. It

wouldn't open. They started back up the corridor. At the foot of the main stairway, Karolina abruptly set down her case and the life belts next to a trunk someone had left behind. "Wait for me, please," she said, and ran back the way they had come.

Gavin stood, staring as she slid to stop in front of cabin eighty-nine. She began beating on the door, calling out for someone named Emily. When the door opened, her voice quieted, and he couldn't understand what she was saying.

"That's our trunk," a sharp-toned woman's voice startled him from above. He faced the stairs. Without another word, two women positioned themselves and began dragging the trunk upward.

"I have to wait for someone," Gavin said apologetically, "or I'd help you." Neither of them acknowledged him. It wasn't until they were nearly out of sight that he realized one of them had taken Karolina's life belts. He shouted, but it did no good.

Gavin saw Karolina hurrying toward him.

She banged on every door she passed. "The ship is sinking," she yelled, over and over. People stepped out into the corridor in their nightclothes, blinking, half-awake. Gavin saw a man he recognized as a pantryman going from one family to the next, talking earnestly. Gavin picked up Karolina's case and followed her up the stairs.

If they were lucky, they would get to the boat deck in time. He could get Karolina and her aunt into one of the lifeboats. Then he would have to find a life belt for himself. He refused to think further than that.

Karolina wanted to run up the stairs, but she couldn't. The case was too heavy. Gavin reached to help her. "Two women took your life belts before I could stop them," he said. Karolina blinked, feeling her stomach tighten. "I know where they are kept," Gavin assured her. "I can get more."

"Karolina!"

She turned back and saw Emily blinking in the bright corridor lights below. Her hair was loose, her nightgown hastily covered with a robe. She held the front of it closed so tightly that her knuckles were white.

"Karolina? Did you see where Davey went?"

Karolina shook her head helplessly. "Wasn't he in the stateroom just now?"

Emily pushed her hair back out of her face, glancing around, her eyes wide with anxiety. "Yes, but you know how he is. Oh, God. I have to find him." She spun back around.

Gavin leaned closer. "Who's Davey? Her son?"

"He's only four," Karolina told Gavin. "He loves to run off."

"Where could he have gone so quickly?" Emily wailed.

Karolina looked at Gavin. "I should go help her look for him."

Gavin nodded. "I'll watch your things. But hurry. I don't know how much time we have."

Karolina set down her case and ran back down the half flight of stairs. Emily was almost all the way back to her stateroom before Karolina caught up.

"He couldn't have gone very far," Karolina

said as Emily pulled the door open. Little Rebecca was still asleep on her berth.

"Oh, why does he have to do this?" Emily said in a tight, frightened voice.

Karolina took her hand. "We'll find him, don't worry."

Emily turned back into the corridor, closing the door carefully. Her eyes flickered to one side, then the other. "I can't believe he got past me. I was just so sleepy—and then all of a sudden I realized he was gone."

"You go that way," Karolina said, pointing. "I'll take the other way." Emily nodded and checked the door to make sure it was solidly closed. Then she started off, turning left down the main passage.

Karolina walked quickly in the other direction, then almost immediately slowed as she passed stateroom sixty-one's open door. "Davey?" She peered inside. "Hello," she said to the couple standing beside their berth. "I was just—"

"What do you want?" the man demanded.

"I'm not going without you," the woman was

saying to him. "Why won't they let the men go?"

"We're going to be all right," he answered her, glaring at Karolina.

Karolina shrugged apologetically. "Have you seen a little boy with dark curly hair?"

The man's face changed dramatically. He looked into her eyes. "You have lost a little brother?"

"A friend's child," Karolina told him.

He shook his head. "I have seen no little boys," he said. "Do you know what is wrong with the ship?"

Karolina took a deep breath. "I think it's going to sink. You should get up to the boat deck." As the man embraced his weeping wife, Karolina turned away.

Most of the doors were closed, but Karolina could hear more and more voices. As she passed the locked stairwell, she reached out and tried the door once more, but it held fast. The main stairs were going to get crowded, Karolina knew. Maybe someone would be down to open these eventually.

"Davey?" she called, then took a breath and

shouted louder. She reached out and touched the wall, suddenly feeling slightly off-balance. She shoved herself forward, barely avoiding two people who stepped suddenly in front of her from room fifty-six. The woman was wrinkled and faltering. The man looked younger. They had on thick woolen coats and were carrying baskets with wooden handles. Karolina asked them if they had seen Davey. They both looked at her with kindly expressions, but neither answered. She repeated the question, but they only shook their heads. Embarrassed that she hadn't understood more quickly that they spoke no English, Karolina walked on.

She turned down one of the narrower corridors that ran at right angles to the main passage. "Davey?" she called. Davey!"

The doors were all closed except one that stood ajar. Karolina knocked upon it, but there was no answer. The strange feeling of dizziness came over her again as she knocked a second time. Still, no one answered. She pushed the door open cautiously. "Davey?"

There was a sudden babble of voices from

farther up the corridor. Karolina looked up and saw a family coming out of their stateroom. They were all so blond their hair looked almost white. The parents were each carrying a small child. Three little boys walked close to their mother's skirt. They all looked terrified.

As they got closer, Karolina stepped into the open doorway to let them pass. Once she was inside, she looked around. There was no one inside the cabin. The berths were rumpled, but there was no luggage—and no Davey.

"Karolina, where are you?"

At the sound of Gavin's voice, Karolina whirled. "Here!" she shouted, stepping awkwardly back into the corridor. Gavin was walking toward her.

"I put your cases in your room. I'll help. Tell me where to start."

Karolina gestured. "Back that way. I was heading toward the stairs. Have you seen Emily?"

Gavin shrugged. "No. But I could hear her calling when I went by with the cases. So she hasn't found him."

Karolina took a step and felt herself leaning

to one side. She stopped, shaking her head. "Something is wrong with my balance. I feel like I can't walk straight."

"It isn't you. The ship is listing to starboard," Gavin said.

Karolina stared at him. "Listing?"

Gavin nodded. "It just means the ship is tilting a little."

Even though he was trying to keep his fear out of his voice, Karolina could hear it. She swallowed hard. "We have to find Davey and get out of here. Aunt Rose is going to be frantic."

"We'll find him," Gavin said, and Karolina could hear the unsteadiness in his voice again.

A crashing sound from inside the cabin made them both turn. Karolina shook her head, puzzled. "I was just in there. I didn't see anyone."

Gavin reached past her to knock on the door as he pushed it open again. "Is someone there?"

Karolina followed him inside. The berths were empty. She turned in a circle, looking at the blank walls, the stark white commode. For the first time she noticed a small passage leading off the main room.

"What's that?" She pointed. "Our stateroom doesn't have anything like that."

Gavin was listening, his head tipped to one side. "It leads to a porthole," he told her.

Karolina stepped forward, acutely aware of the weird slant of the floor, extending one hand to trace the shape of the angled wall as she went. For a moment, she thought no one was there. Then she heard Davey singing to himself, and she felt tears spring into her eyes.

He was standing on a stool, his nose pressed against the glass. "Hello, Karolina," he said quietly. "Is my mama upset with me?"

"She'll just be glad to see you," Karolina assured him. Then she raised her voice and called out to Gavin. She picked Davey up, and he perched on her hip, his arms around her neck. She ducked to glance out the porthole and caught her breath. The crooked horizon line was marked by bright stars. Karolina stared for a few seconds. The *Titanic* really was going to sink.

CHAPTER NINE

As Karolina handed Davey over to his mother, Gavin stood uneasily, a case in each hand. The slant of the deck made him feel sick with fear. If the ship was listing, it meant that it was taking on more water.

"I'll come up to the boat deck as soon as I can get the children dressed," Emily was saying. "God bless you for helping."

Karolina's face was full of concern. "Are you sure you'll be all right?" she asked.

Gavin watched Emily nod. "You go ahead. Don't make Rose wait."

Gavin led the way toward the third–class entrance, walking as fast as he could. There were more people on the stairs this time, most of them carrying boxes or dragging trunks. It was hard to maneuver through them. Once they were out of the worst of the crowd, Gavin nodded at Karolina. "You were brave to help Emily."

Karolina's eyes caught his and held. "Are we really going to sink, Gavin? Do you think we are going to die?" She whispered it, glancing back down the stairs.

Gavin shook his head. "There will be rescue ships here soon. Maybe they're here now."

"I saw them sending up flares," Karolina said as they rounded the first landing. A family was standing there. Three little children were leaning sleepily against their mother's skirt. The father, a balding man who still looked half-asleep, was talking loudly to his wife.

"I'm telling you, they don't want us up there," he was saying. "The steward said it's all for the first-class passengers, and that we are to wait here."

"But we have to go somewhere," his wife sniffled. Her hair was loose, tumbling down her back. "We're going to die. Oh, dear God, I'm scared."

Gavin led Karolina around them, trying not to hear any more of the woman's panicked words. He could feel his own fear thundering in every heartbeat. "Listen to your wife, Mister," he said, turning back. "You have to get up to the boat deck." The woman looked angrily at her husband, and they began to argue.

The stairs seemed endlessly long this time. The case Gavin carried was heavy. He kept glancing back at Karolina. She was managing to keep up. Gavin looked toward the top of the stairs and shook his head. They seemed steep. Too steep.

Struggling up onto the landing, Gavin stopped, blinking, unable to believe his eyes.

"It's slanting, like you said," Karolina breathed, close behind him. There was both wonder and terror in her voice. And she was right. The *Titanic* was tipped dangerously forward, her bow lowering under the weight of the water that had poured into it.

Gavin stared into the darkness of the sky for a moment, at the ice-shard stars flickering above his head. Then he let his eyes come back to the little section of deck that served as the third-class promenade. It was slanting markedly downward, away from them.

He picked up the case again, looking back toward the door as someone behind them cried out. A knot of confused voices tangled together in the cold air. Astonished, he realized that he could hear the band, still playing quick-rhythmed ragtime.

"Come with me," he said to Karolina. Her eyes were unfocused. He repeated it, louder. She nodded and lifted her case, gesturing for him to go first. Gavin had to step around groups of people who stood near the foot of the stairs that led up to B-deck, some talking intently, some silent.

He leaned into the incline of the deck, fighting a sense of unreality. It was as strange as if the ground beneath his mother's house had suddenly taken a whim to tilt. Gavin's shoes skidded, and he glanced back at Karolina. She looked pale and stricken, but she was still keeping up.

"This way," Gavin called to her, starting up

the steps. He gripped the handrail, hauling himself upward, his feet sliding forward on the stair treads that now slanted sharply toward the bow of the ship.

Just as they reached the top, a crewman Gavin didn't recognize pulled a gate closed behind them. He locked it, then strode away without looking back. Gavin saw people on the well deck below looking up, their faces marked with panic and anger.

"How can they do that? What about Emily?" Karolina asked.

Gavin could only shake his head. "I don't know, Karolina."

Tears wet her cheeks, and he could see her fighting to stay calm. "Aunt Rose told me she would wait here," she said very slowly, clearing her throat when her voice caught. Her face was a mask of dismay, and she kept glancing at the people on the other side of the gate.

Gavin looked around the little corner of B-deck, setting the case down beside a group of passengers who were standing close together. The women all had bright silk parasols in their hands. Their life belts were fastened over thick woolen coats. Gavin looked past them. A flare exploded, then streaked its way back down toward the sea. It winked out as he watched.

"She isn't here," Karolina was saying.

Gavin faced her. "Are you sure?"

Karolina scowled. "I know what my aunt looks like, Gavin." Her face changed instantly. "I'm sorry. I just can't stop thinking about Emily. And I'm so scared."

Gavin nodded. "I am, too." He glanced toward the boat deck above them. "Your aunt probably just went up there. That's where any steward would tell her to go."

Karolina nodded at him. Together they made their way toward the second-class stairs. They didn't stop on A-deck but kept going until they emerged into the cold air again. Gavin stared out at the black water on all sides of the ship. His stomach clenched.

At that moment, the deck beneath their feet began to tremble, and Gavin felt it tilt even more toward the bow. He looked aft, his breath catching in his throat—it was as if the stern was going to lift up out of the water. The poop deck was full of people. He could see piles of clothing and trunks scattered across it.

Gavin took Karolina's hand, fighting his own panic. "Come on. Let's find your aunt." Feeling light and strange, hearing the opening strains of a waltz, Gavin forced himself to go toward the lifeboats. Most of them had been lowered and were swinging gently from their davits.

"Where could she be?" Karolina asked as they walked past the first few lifeboats.

He shrugged. "Some of the boats are already gone. Maybe she's in one of them."

Karolina looked offended, then terrified. "She wouldn't leave me."

Gavin touched her cheek. "Then we'll find her. We just have to keep looking." He scanned the boat deck. There were hundreds of well-dressed people standing in groups, stamping their feet against the cold. The women's hands were tucked inside mink and ermine muffs or warmed by kid leather gloves. Here and there, steerage families stood together. Gavin imagined his brothers and sisters, all scared, huddling close for warmth. He thought about the locked gate and shuddered.

"I didn't know there were this many people aboard," Karolina said quietly, interrupting his thoughts.

Gavin stared at the crowd, then looked back at the remaining lifeboats. He turned, forcing himself to look out to sea. There were no other ships close by. He felt an ache of fear claw its way down his spine.

"Are you all right, Gavin?"

Gavin shook his head, but he didn't answer her. He blinked, looking out at the dark, cold ocean. Where were the rescue ships? There weren't nearly enough lifeboats to hold everyone.

CHAPTER TEN

Karolina shivered. Her teeth were chattering partly from fear, partly because she was so cold. All around them were crowds of frightened people. Karolina scanned their faces, expecting, hoping, that she would see her aunt. Children were crying, and she could hear someone's lapdog yipping, a high, irritating noise. The band was playing beautiful, precise music now—an odd partner for the hubbub of voices.

For a strange instant, Karolina wondered if anyone was dancing. Normally, it wasn't permitted on Sunday nights on the ship, but surely no one would be bothering anyone who wanted to waltz now.

Gavin nudged her elbow. "Can you see your aunt? What does she look like?"

Karolina shook her head. "She's tall. Her hat has a big silk rose in the band." She looked back toward the second-class entrance, feeling lost. Why had Aunt Rose moved? She had said she would wait right there. Maybe it had gotten too crowded. Maybe she had come up here to get them a place in a lifeboat.

Karolina scanned the fear-tensed faces. They looked like people out of a dream. Some of the women were still dressed in their formal gowns. Others wore nightclothes. One woman wore a purple silk dress—but no shoes or stockings. Many of the others had left their shoes behind in their hurry to get up here. Their stockings were dark with coal dust.

"We should check the port side," Gavin said. "Half the lifeboats are over there." He gestured.

Karolina watched him fidget. "Maybe," she said reluctantly, unable to stop looking toward the second-class entrance. "I just can't believe she wouldn't wait for me."

"Karolina? Is that you?"

Karolina turned to see Emily struggling to keep her balance on the slanting deck. Rebecca was straddling her hip. Davey walked stiff-kneed, his hand enclosed in his mother's tight grasp.

Karolina ran toward them. "They locked the gate. How did you get up here?"

"Remember the locked door across from your room? A steward opened it. Twenty or thirty of us came up together."

Karolina hugged Emily, then stepped back. "I can't find Aunt Rose."

"It's possible she's already in a lifeboat," Gavin said quietly, pointing. "Some of the ones farther up have already been lowered." He squinted. "Maybe all of them."

Karolina shook her head. "She wouldn't leave me."

"Are we supposed to just wait?" Emily asked Gavin.

Karolina watched as he looked up and down the boat deck. "That's First Officer Murdoch up there. He would know."

"I think people are just lining up," Karolina said.

Ahead of them were clusters of passengers standing in loose groups alongside each lifeboat. Uniformed crew members were shouting, trying to organize the crowds. No one seemed to be panicking, at least not yet. Karolina turned to look once more toward the corner of the deck where Aunt Rose had promised to wait.

"I'm going to see if we can get on now," Emily said. "You two come with me."

Gavin shook his head. "I should be helping."

Karolina met Emily's eyes. "I have to find Aunt Rose first."

Emily hugged her again. Rebecca made a little squeal of delight to be sandwiched between them. Davey smiled at Karolina when she ruffled his hair.

"We'll all meet again either on the rescue ships or in New York," Emily said, smiling bravely.

Karolina watched her walk away, making her way through the crowds. When Emily got close enough for a steward to see her, he waved her forward, helping her step over the railing, lifting Davey into the boat for her.

The deck shuddered beneath their feet, and the lifeboat swung back and forth. Karolina saw Davey look up, startled. Emily lurched to one side. Karolina stumbled against Gavin, but managed to keep her balance by catching hold of his arm. As she straightened, she saw the look of wide-eyed fear on his face. She followed his gaze and, in spite of the bitter cold, she felt a clammy sweat on the back of her neck—the stern of the ship had risen in the water. "Why is that happening, Gavin?"

He shook his head. "Maybe the bow is filling up with water. You should get into that lifeboat. Now." He pushed her forward, but she struggled with him, a strange mix of anger and fear rising inside her.

"I have to find Aunt Rose, Gavin. I lost my parents; I can't lose her, too." She began to cry. The whole world had collapsed, everything that she was supposed to be able to count on had disappeared. She bit at her lip and tried to stop the tears, but it was impossible.

"Karolina! Come on, get in!"

Emily was gesturing wildly, and Karolina felt Gavin urging her toward the lifeboat. One of the crewmen was reaching out to help her. Blinking back tears, she twisted wildly and ran away from them all, clumsy and faltering on the tilting deck.

Gavin watched Karolina run away, unable to react for a moment.

"We can't wait for her," one of the crewmen shouted.

Gavin turned to see him pushing Emily back down onto her bench. Emily was arguing with him, pointing in the direction Karolina had run.

"I'll make sure she gets on a boat," Gavin called out.

Emily leaned forward. "Promise me. On your mother's soul."

Gavin nodded. "I will. I'll make sure."

Emily sat down and smiled at him gratefully. "Thank you, young man. God bless you."

The hoists were raising the lifeboat now, and Emily swayed with the motion, clutching her children as the boat swung out over the black water far below. Davey had buried his face in his mother's side. The boat was swinging back and forth on its ropes. Gavin could imagine the fear the little boy felt at hanging so precariously over the water.

Gavin shivered and rubbed his hands together, then made his way back through the people who stood transfixed, watching as the boat was lowered. He excused himself, moving through the middle of what looked like one big family. They all had dark, curly hair and wide blue eyes. One woman held a crying baby. An older man stood behind her, his hands on her shoulders. Quickly, Gavin glanced away, longing for his own family.

He squared his shoulders and started toward the bow. It was hard to walk. The deck was slanting forward, making every step awkward. He scanned the faces he passed, but Karolina was not among them. Nor was Harry. People standing in the darkness of the open deck were much harder to see. The bright lights mounted along the edge of the structures that surrounded the towering funnels and the main entrances illuminated hundreds of faces. None of them was familiar. None of them had a hat with a big silk rose. Every one of them was pale and frightened.

Men were talking in overloud voices. Women cried or laughed, their voices as sharp as glass in the cold air. The band, he realized suddenly, was still playing. This piece was a minor key waltz, slower and more somber than the music that had come before. If the musicians were afraid, they somehow kept it from tainting the beauty of their music.

Gavin hurried. He wove in and out of the crowd, scanning the faces he passed. Finally, he gave up and ducked into the gymnasium, using the same door Lionel had shown them. Once inside, he crossed the crowded landing at the top of the Grand Staircase and came back out onto the deck on the port side.

The band was playing here. A crowd of people had gathered around them, and it took Gavin a few minutes to work his way past. Almost immediately, he spotted Karolina. She was approaching first one group, then another, peering into women's faces as she went.

"Karolina!" Gavin shouted.

She seemed not to hear him. The babble of the crowd was getting louder and louder. Walking toward the stern again, the deck was an incline. Gavin's feet were getting numb. His wet shoes were clammy, and he wished for the dry shoes and socks he had thrown away. His cabin was probably flooded by now. The image of his trunk and his berth immersed in the cold saltwater made him shiver. He looked out into the darkness beyond the ship. There was nothing to protect him from the icy black ocean now.

"Karolina!" he shouted again. This time, she turned and saw him. He stepped around a fur-coated woman who glared at him when he bumped into her arm. "Watch yourself, son," her husband snapped. Then he put his arms around his wife and held her close.

"Gavin? Gavin, did you find my aunt?"

Her face was so full of hope, he hated to answer. "No, Karolina," he said reluctantly.

Suddenly she started shivering, her eyes hollow and scared. "I don't know where she could be. What if she tried to go back down after me?" Her voice broke, and he knew she was fighting tears again.

Gavin shook his head, stamping his feet. "She wouldn't have done that. You said the stairs were too hard for her." He looked toward the port side lifeboats. "The crew is loading women and children first. I'm sure someone already convinced your aunt to get on one of the lifeboats. She's probably fine and worrying about you."

"I don't know. . . ." Karolina's voice was tight with indecision.

"You need to get on a lifeboat. I can only see two left on this side, and for all we know, the starboard-side boats are already gone. This could be your only chance."

"How much time do you think we have, Gavin?"

Gavin shook his head. "I don't know."

He had barely finished speaking when he felt the deck shift again. The incline steepened once more. Karolina cried out, and he steadied her, forcing her forward, pulling her up the sloping deck. Ahead of them, a woman screamed—the sound cut off abruptly. Gavin couldn't see what had happened, but lifeboat number two was now swinging from its davits.

"Oh, God," Karolina whispered.

Gavin grasped her elbow and guided her around a group of men dressed in dark suits. They were grim, silent, standing almost shoulder to shoulder, staring out to sea. Gavin looked back at the lifeboat and suddenly understood. There were no men aboard except the crew. Women sat on the benches, some weeping, some blank-faced. Some of them held small children on their laps.

"We have more seats!" a crew member shouted into the crowd.

"Here!" Gavin called back. He gestured at Karolina and saw the man nod.

"What if Aunt Rose is—" Karolina began.

"She would want you to save yourself," Gavin interrupted, hurrying her through the last ragged line of couples who stood looking on. Some of the women were sobbing openly.

None of them seemed eager to step forward and get on the lifeboat.

Gavin understood why. They did not want to leave their husbands. Besides, it was hard to believe that the wide, solid deck of the *Titanic* was less safe than a flimsy wooden lifeboat. If Lionel hadn't told him the truth, if he hadn't seen the water pouring in with his own eyes, Gavin wasn't sure he would believe it, either. He glanced over the side and forced himself to look at the black water.

"How long before the distress signals are answered?" a man shouted out.

The officer in the bow of the lifeboat raised his head. "I have no way to know, sir. It ought to be any time now. These shipping lanes are busy this time of year."

"It's better to stay onboard," a man near Gavin said loudly. He took his wife's arm, and they moved back. Gavin pulled Karolina forward.

"Gavin?"

He looked up to see Lionel staggering under a load of life preservers.

"Give me a hand with these, will you? Make

sure anyone you see has one on. Some of the men are refusing to take them. Argue with them if you can." Lionel nodded at Karolina, then slid the stack of life preservers down his arm.

Gavin caught half a dozen of them, and Lionel clapped him on the shoulder as he straightened. "Thanks, Gavin. With any luck, we'll all be telling this story the rest of our lives." He grinned, then paced away.

"Right this way, young lady," the crewman was shouting at Karolina. "Hurry now, please. And the woman back there? Yes, you," he shouted over Gavin's head. Gavin glanced back to see a young couple kissing farewell.

"Step up now, we're about to lower the boat," the crewman snapped. "This is a cutter, folks; it won't hold as many as the big boats."

Karolina hesitated, and Gavin hitched the life preservers higher. They were awkward and heavy. "Karolina, you have to get on now. Take one of these."

She took the life belt, but didn't put it on. "I can't just go without—"

"Yes, you can," Gavin said. "You must."

Karolina frowned. "*I* must? What about you?"

"Come on, Miss," the crewman said. "Get on now, or you will be left behind."

Gavin watched Karolina lift her chin and peer into the boat. "Gavin, you have to come, too. There are crewmen on every boat we've seen and—"

"Let us pass, please," a voice demanded from behind them.

Karolina stepped aside. Gavin made way for a big man who escorted two young women to the boat rail. They sobbed as they got in, and the man stood a few seconds, holding their hands across the little gap that separated the lifeboat from the deck. Then he spun around and walked away without looking back. The two young women sank onto the boat benches, watching him go.

Karolina faced Gavin. "You can come with me. The boat isn't nearly full. They'll let you on."

Gavin pulled in a deep breath. "Almost none

of the men are going, Karolina. I have to stay. I'll look around for your aunt and I'll make sure she gets a life belt. If help comes, we'll all be fine. And it probably will. You heard Lionel."

Gavin pushed her forward. If he argued with her much longer, he was afraid his cowardice would win out over his courage. "Karolina?" He reached into his pocket and pulled out the photograph of his family. "My brother's name is Conor Reilly, and he lives in New York City. He's a cabinetmaker. Find him, will you? And give him this. Tell him I love him. Tell him to write our mother."

He extended the photograph, and Karolina took it, her hand shaking. She tucked it inside her bodice. Then, before he could move away, she put her arms around his neck and hugged him.

He turned her around, waiting until the crewman had hold of her hand before he moved back. He watched the man lift the life preserver over her head and tie it tightly across her chest.

Gavin stood very still, the cold night air

seeping into his heart. He was terrified of the dark water and he knew that was part of the reason he didn't want to get into the lifeboat. But it was more than that. He refused to be a coward. Lionel was somewhere, doing his job. So was most of the rest of the crew. They weren't scrambling to get in the lifeboats. Nor were most of the other men onboard.

Gavin began handing out the life belts. The last two he gave to a family who didn't speak English. He helped them tie the straps around a wriggling toddler. As they thanked him, he felt incredibly alone.

There were so many things Gavin wanted to say to his mother. He wished he had given Karolina a message for each of his brothers and sisters. Why hadn't he thought of that?

But even as he asked himself the question, he knew the answer. Until this moment, he had believed he was somehow going to live through this awful night. Now, he wasn't sure at all.

CHAPTER ELEVEN

"Lower away!"

Karolina heard the crewman's cry and felt the first tiny shift of the lifeboat at almost the same instant. The curved arms, where the pulleys were set, rose gracefully overhead, silhouetted by the brightly burning deck lights.

"Stay together, now. Mind what I say," the crewman shouted as the men on the winches set to work.

Karolina steeled herself as the lifeboat jerked a few inches to the side, then swung back, bumping the deck. She could still see Gavin, standing with his arms crossed over his chest for warmth. She shivered, wishing she could think of some way to thank him, some way to. . . .

"Don't worry, we'll be all right, honey."

Karolina looked up into the face of a well-dressed, gray-haired woman. "I can't find my aunt," Karolina said, without realizing that she was going to say it. Her voice sounded high and uneven in her own ears. The boat jerked again. Karolina saw Gavin wave, and she waved back. The band finished one song and began another.

"God bless you and keep you always," the woman next to her murmured. "I will love you forever, my darling."

Karolina glanced at her and realized she was whispering, the words intended for a spectacled man who stood watching the lifeboat be lowered. He had both hands in his pockets, and his shoulders were hunched against the freezing night air.

"If you can spare him, Lord, I will do anything," the woman whispered, then she began to recite the Lord's Prayer, over and over, her eyes closed as the lifeboat swayed over the open water.

Karolina's eyes ached with tears as she stared at Gavin. He was standing straight and tall, and his head was high. This was even more awful for him than for most people, she knew. She wanted, more than anything, to make the boat stop, to force the crewmen to let Gavin come aboard. Gavin waved once more, a tiny motion of his hand.

"I'll find your brother, Gavin," Karolina shouted to him. He nodded, an exaggerated gesture so she could see him and understand. "And I'll see you in New York," she added. Her voice was rough and strained, and she hoped he couldn't hear how terrified she was.

The boat lurched, and Karolina gripped the edge of the seat with both hands. The gray-haired woman was still praying, her whisper as constant as a summer breeze through tall grass. Karolina leaned forward, trying to maintain eye contact with Gavin, but the boat was moving downward now, and after a moment, she could see only the yellowish light pouring from inside the staterooms and saloons.

In the suddenly bright light, Karolina

looked at the passengers in the boat. Some of the women were wearing furs and more glittering jewelry than she had ever seen before. Others were dressed much more plainly. One woman had forgotten her shoes in her hurry to leave the *Titanic*. All the men in the boat were wearing uniforms. Karolina glanced wildly upward, anger rising in her heart. Why hadn't they let Gavin come aboard? Why hadn't he even tried?

The boat tilted forward, and Karolina heard the woman beside her pull in a quick, startled breath.

"Lower stern!" a shout came from a man in the bow. The winches creaked, and the rope made a high, whining noise as it ran through the pulleys. The boat leveled, then overcorrected, the stern sinking so low that Karolina had to lean forward.

"Lower bow!" the shout rose in unison from two or three of the crewmen.

Again the pulleys shrieked and groaned as the winches strained. The lifeboat was lowered again, the lighted portholes sliding past on one side. Karolina caught a glimpse of a dog's face, its mouth open as if it were barking against the glass. Then it was gone, and she was peering into a room with trunks and cases spilled out onto the floor. As the boat slid down past more lighted portholes, she saw people standing in a small circle, their arms around each other.

"Lower bow!"

The shout came before Karolina even noticed that the boat was tilting again. The glassy black water below them was coming closer and closer. The *Titanic* towered above her now, seeming impossibly big—like a city that had somehow been flung into the ocean.

"Good-bye, my love," the woman next to her whispered, and Karolina saw her looking upward.

The lifeboat swung gently from its ropes, moving downward. The ocean, dark and endless, reflected the eerie brightness of the stars. Karolina felt herself shiver and she looked back up toward the boat deck. She couldn't see Gavin anymore, but she could imagine his fear. Tears flooded her eyes.

"It's all right, dear," the gray-haired woman said quietly. "We'll be just fine. I was told that rescue ships are on their way."

Karolina smiled politely and scanned the horizon. The only lights that broke up the dark sky were stars. There were no rescue ships.

"Gavin!"

Gavin turned to see Lionel running toward him on the slanting deck, still carrying a stack of life preservers. "Are we really going down, Lionel?" Gavin asked without meaning to.

Lionel nodded somberly. "I think so. A first-class steward told me that Mr. Andrews said so."

Gavin blinked. "Mr. Andrews?"

Lionel set down all but one of the life preservers. "Mr. Andrews is one of the builders. He should know."

Gavin glanced out at the glassy black water. His heart was pounding against his ribs. It was going to get him, after all. The water was going to get him.

"Here. Gavin? You should have saved one for yourself."

Gavin looked back at Lionel, unable to focus on what he was saying.

"Put it on, Gavin."

Gavin took the life preserver, then he held it loosely in his hands. After a few seconds, the printed messages on the life belt began to make sense to him. INSIDE FRONT, INSIDE BACK. He turned the preserver so that it would go on straight, then lifted it over his head.

"Get forward now, Gavin," Lionel was saying. "Get on one of the collapsibles if you can."

"Have you heard anything? Is help coming?" Gavin asked, his voice shaky. He pulled in a deep breath and concentrated on tying the life preserver straps across his chest and belly.

"The cork in this will keep you afloat for a long time," Lionel said.

Gavin nodded and swallowed hard. His throat was so tight with fear, he couldn't answer.

Lionel pointed toward the bridge. "Get up there. Maybe you can get a place."

"What about you?"

Lionel shook his head. "Look." He gestured, a wide, sweeping motion with his right hand. "There are hundreds of us here."

Gavin nodded, shaking with cold and nervousness. The crowd was quieting now, with only a little round of gasps each time the bow dropped lower in the water. The band, he realized, astounded, was still playing.

"Go on, now," Lionel interrupted his thoughts. "Collapsible D is on this side, up by the bridge. And if you see Harry, get him on it, too."

"Come with me, Lionel."

Lionel shook his head. "I want to get down to D-deck if I can. I think there are people still down there. I saw men climbing the hoists to get up here."

Gavin stared at him. "They locked the gate coming up from the well deck."

"If they are up on deck, they have a chance," Lionel said. "The Marconi operator has been sending a distress signal for hours. If a ship does come along, we might all make it yet." He reached out and clapped Gavin on the shoulder, then started off through the crowds.

The deck shuddered beneath Gavin's feet,

and he nearly fell. The slope was sharper all the time. He looked out across the water and was shocked to see how much closer it looked now. The bow was filling with water so quickly that there might be little time left.

Gavin started toward the lifeboat Lionel had pointed out. It was above the boat deck, fixed to the roof of the wheelhouse. Men were up there now, kneeling beside it. Someone had placed narrow ramps extending from beneath the boat to the boat deck below. As Gavin watched, the boat was skidded down them and ropes attached to it.

The downward slope of the deck was steep enough to make it hard to walk without stumbling into people. Just ahead Gavin saw a heavyset boy in a White Star uniform struggling with a bulging burlap bag. As Gavin got closer, he recognized Wallace.

"What are you doing?" Gavin demanded as he caught up.

Wallace looked startled, then almost angry. "What do you care?"

Gavin shrugged. "Lionel told me to get on

that lifeboat." He pointed at the collapsible. People were climbing into it now. "Do you know where Harry is?"

Wallace hoisted the bag higher on his back, grunting with effort. "I haven't seen him." He gestured at the lifeboat. "Do you think they'd let me on, too?"

Gavin nodded. "Why not? Maybe not that bag, though. What's in it, Wallace?"

Wallace looked up at the stars, then met Gavin's eyes again. "Swear you won't tell anyone?" He set the bag down.

Gavin frowned. "Tell me later. I want to get on that lifeboat."

Gavin started off, glancing back, realizing that the bag was so heavy Wallace could barely lift it. "Leave it here."

Wallace looked offended. "I can't."

"How badly do you want to live?" Gavin asked him. He pointed. The collapsible was close to half full now. "Come on."

Wallace lagged behind. Gavin was in line while Wallace was still fighting the heavy bag down the inclined deck. Wallace fell in beside a family with two small children—both crying. Their mother, a soft-spoken woman with a musical voice, kept trying to reassure them. Their father, tears streaming down his face, was urging his wife forward, his arm protectively around her shoulders.

"We have room for seven more," a crewman near the collapsible cried out to the crowd. A soft chorus of moans went up as four women quickly stepped forward and got on.

Gavin was just behind them, looking at the people already seated in the boat. There were men here, though not as many as women. Still, there didn't seem to be a hard-and-fast rule. He scanned the crowd. Harry was nowhere to be seen—nor was Karolina's aunt.

"Three more!"

Gavin glanced back at Wallace, trying to catch his eye. Wallace's whole attention was on the bag he carried. He was leaning into its weight, gripping the top like his life depended on keeping it.

"Three more!" the crewman shouted again.

Gavin stepped forward at the same moment

that the man in back of him shepherded his wife and children closer to the boat. Gavin looked at them. The little girl was weeping, obviously terrified. Her brother had stopped crying, but his face was pinched and pale.

The man caught Gavin's eye and mouthed a single word. "Please."

Thinking about his own sisters and brothers, Gavin moved aside. He heard people behind him arguing about what they ought to do now that this boat was filled. Two or three groups started off, almost running. Gavin knew what they were doing. They hoped the other collapsibles on the starboard side weren't yet full.

"Gavin?"

He turned to see Wallace dragging the bag toward him. For the first time, he noticed that Wallace wasn't wearing a life belt. Involuntarily, he glanced in the direction Lionel had gone, carrying the pile of preservers. "Where's your life belt, Wallace?" he asked, beginning to understand.

"I left it down below. I got this, instead."

Wallace laughed quietly and nudged the bag with his foot.

"A life belt is worth more than anything you have in that bag, Wallace."

"You're crazy, Gavin. I will never have to work again."

The angle of the deck beneath their feet increased suddenly, and Gavin whirled to look out at the water.

"Lower away!" the crewman shouted frantically. The collapsible lifeboat swung outward.

Gavin's stomach clenched. The water was no longer far below. It was barely ten feet from where he stood. The *Titanic* was sinking fast.

CHAPTER TWELVE

The ropes squealed through the pulleys, and Karolina sat rigidly, trying not to think about the icy ocean below. In a few seconds, the lifeboat would be bobbing on the glassy surface. She shivered. It was so cold.

"Is the plug in place?" one of the crewmen was shouting. "We don't want to take on water."

There was a scramble near the bow of the boat. A seaman half-stood, muttering. Karolina watched him work his way, crouching, to the center of the boat. He bent over, and she could see him straining to do something.

"Got it," he finally said, straightening enough to make his way back to his seat.

As the lifeboat touched the surface of the water, Karolina felt an odd weightlessness, then a soft rocking motion.

"Man the oars!"

The order was given by an officer in the bow. A crewman wrestled the oars into the oarlocks one at a time, moving awkwardly between the passengers.

"We're ready, Officer Boxhall," he said when he was finished.

"I can help row," a woman said from one bench back.

Karolina turned to look at her. She wasn't young, but her face was determined, and she gave off an aura of calm and strength.

"I know how to row," another woman said from the stern.

"And I," came a third voice.

There was a slow changing of seats, Officer Boxhall directing their movements so that the boat was not too much disturbed. Then two crewmen and the women began to row. Karolina suddenly noticed a bearded man near the bow who kept up a murmur in a language

Karolina didn't recognize. It sounded like a prayer, and she hoped that it was.

"When she goes down, there'll be a wave that could swamp us," Officer Boxhall called to the rowers. "Or an undertow. So put your backs into it, men, and ladies, if you are able."

Karolina only half-heard what he was saying as the lifeboat began to move away from the *Titanic*. Everyone was staring at the enormous vessel. It was strange to see the giant ship lying docilely at a slant in the water. The brightly lit portholes, arranged in their neat rows, met the black surface of the water at an angle. It was like seeing train tracks meet: It was wrong, impossible.

The lights fascinated Karolina. She wondered if the ones below the waterline were still burning. She imagined the first-class staterooms fully lit, people's belongings still neatly arranged in the closets and on the shelves. The water would seep in soon, cold and relentless. Was Gavin still aboard? Where was Aunt Rose? Karolina bit at her lip, hard, trying to still the painful thoughts.

"Row harder, if you can. She'll be going

down soon, and the wave could easily catch us if we are this close."

Karolina heard one of the women begin to cry, a soft, racking sound. The older woman next to Karolina was sitting up very straight, her chin held high.

The *Titanic* tilted forward again, and there were odd, haunted groans from the ship's metal hull. There were screams from the open boat deck. Karolina looked up. Astonished, she saw hundreds of people still onboard. Many of them were hurrying toward the rising stern even as they cried out. Karolina shuddered, listening as the commotion rose, then fell back into silence as the *Titanic* settled into its awkward new position.

At first the rowers worked hard, and the lifeboat cut through the calm water. Once they were some distance away from the *Titanic*, they slowed, then stopped rowing, staring back at the ship. Karolina sat very still in the half-empty lifeboat. No one was talking. They were all silent, helpless, watching the *Titanic*. In the darkness, the little cutter rocked on the glassy surface.

"Oh, my God," the woman next to her breathed.

"Row, port side. Starboard, ship your oars," Officer Boxhall shouted.

"He means lift your oar up out of the water," Karolina heard one of the women explaining to someone. "The boat will turn if only one side is rowing."

Karolina twisted on her seat to look. It was true. They were curving back toward the *Titanic* in a slow arc.

"Starboard side, oars back in the water!" Officer Boxhall called. "I want to come around the stern. Maybe we can get close enough to her starboard side to take on a few more people."

As they rowed, Karolina could see the crowds swarming over the poop deck and the stern. Even the well deck, where Davey had run from her, laughing, was now full of frightened people.

Karolina blinked, digging her fingernails into the wooden bench. There were children her own age looking down at her. There were men, perched high on the cargo cranes, clinging with one hand and waving desperately with the other. She could see their faces.

The *Titanic* was nosing into the water now, its bow so much lower than its stern that it was disorienting to look at it. Karolina squeezed her eyes shut, then turned her head before she opened them again and looked out at the vast, menacing ocean. There were no ships close by. She was sure of it. Their lights would have been visible for miles on this clear night.

It was so dark. The stars were a canopy of sparkling pinpoints, more beautiful and peaceful than anything she had ever seen. She looked up at them and thought about her parents. Her eyes flooded, and she said a silent prayer for Aunt Rose and Gavin.

As the lifeboat neared the stern, Karolina saw that there were more people crowded along the promenades now. She craned her neck, trying to see their faces. Was Gavin among them? Or Aunt Rose? She thought she could see Lionel, his tall, thin frame braced against the rail, his blond hair windblown.

"Port oars out of the water," Officer Boxhall commanded.

The boat turned, rounding the stern of the *Titanic*. The giant propellers were half out of the water. The sea sloshed in little eddies around the exposed rudder.

"All oars back in. Keep straight on."

The boat shuddered, then straightened as the inexperienced women found a rhythm in their efforts. Karolina leaned forward, still scanning the crowds, searching the faces. The lifeboat drew closer and closer. Karolina could hear voices across the open stretch of water between the ship and the lifeboat.

"Ship oars!" Officer Boxhall commanded.

Karolina jerked around to stare at him. As the lifeboat glided to a stop in the water, Officer Boxhall leaned forward, a look of fear on his face.

"What are you doing?" one of the older women demanded.

"I am afraid there is some suction already," Officer Boxhall said. "It could draw us right down with it."

"But we can't just leave all those people—" Karolina began.

"If we lose twenty-five to save one, that's not right," a crewman said when Officer Boxhall did not answer.

"We could go a little closer," Karolina argued. "We could just see if. . . ." She trailed off, realizing she was speaking so quietly that Officer Boxhall could not possibly have heard her. The woman sitting beside her took her hand and held it silently. Karolina remembered the woman's husband, how brave and strong he had seemed.

"Our husbands and sons wouldn't want us put into more danger," a woman said from the stern.

Officer Boxhall shouted orders, and the rowers fumblingly complied. Within a few moments, the boat was moving away from the *Titanic* again. Tears blurring her vision, Karolina watched helplessly as the faces on the stern became smaller with distance, then impossible to see.

Finally, once they were well away, Officer Boxhall had the rowers ship their oars again.

The lifeboat glided forward a little longer, then came to a swaying stop. The lights on the *Titanic* were still burning brightly, and Karolina was sure she could still hear the distant sound of music.

Officer Boxhall called for another rocket and lit the fuse, sending it off into the night sky. The green ball of fire soared above them, arcing very slowly back down to the black water. Karolina saw it hit, its light instantly extinguished.

A thin sound of distant screaming made Karolina jerk back around. The *Titanic* was pitching forward. Karolina could see people hanging on to railings, clinging to each other and whatever came to hand. As she stared, horrified, she saw several people fall, all at once, sliding across the deck, then overboard, into the sea. One man seemed to run at the rail, jumping outward from the side of the ship.

The squeal of the tortured metal was almost unbearable. Then, as more people dropped from their desperate perches, the bow dipped even lower. The deck was an incline no one could climb now. From deep inside the ship, Karolina heard a swelling crash, the shrieking of metal being torn by the force of its own weight.

"That's the boilers and the engines letting go," one of the crewmen said quietly. "Everything in her that can fall is crashing straight through the bulkheads now."

Karolina clenched her jaw against the horrible cacophony. She imagined the inside of the ship like an overturned doll house—the furniture, the silver, the thousands of glasses in the dining saloons, the pianos—everything would be destroyed. Then, after what seemed like a long time, the incredible noise stopped, and Karolina realized that the stern was rising, had been rising. The *Titanic* was very nearly vertical, its stern towering far above the surface of the sea.

Standing against the stars like an impossible vision, the huge ship seemed to balance itself on the black water. The lights flickered, then came back on. Finally, in one smooth, incredible slide, the *Titanic* disappeared beneath the ocean. Everything was silent. Then, Karolina could hear the screams.

CHAPTER THIRTEEN

Both Gavin and Wallace had been standing near the rail when Second Officer Lightoller had unholstered his gun. Crewmen had linked arms in case the crowd surged forward, trying to board the Engelhardt boat. The collapsible canvas vessel had been hooked up to the same set of davits that had launched wooden lifeboat number two. Gavin was still scanning the crowd for Karolina's aunt, but he had nearly lost hope of seeing a red rose tucked into a hatband.

"Women, come forward," Lightoller shouted.

Gavin saw an elderly lady and a young girl work their way out of the crowd. They were well dressed. He thought about the women he had seen in third class, dragging their trunks up the stairs. Where were they? Most of this crowd was from second and first class, he was sure.

The lifeboat was lowered slowly, and Gavin watched it ease toward the water. It was more than half full—but there were empty seats on the benches. He could hear a woman's voice talking loudly, insistently, but he couldn't make out her words.

As the boat was lowered past A-deck, Gavin heard a man's shout, then saw him leaping out to land headfirst in the collapsible. A second later another man leaped for safety, but he was less lucky and almost fell into the ocean, hanging on with one hand. The first man scrambled to his feet in time to pull his companion aboard. All around Gavin, people were fighting the slope of the deck. The crowd was scattering. He searched one last time for Harry, then lowered his eyes to the water again.

The canvas boat touched the sea, and the officer in charge was screaming for everyone to fix oars and row away. At that instant, there was an awful groaning sound, as if a giant voice deep within the ship was crying out for help. The pitch of the deck was now so steep that Gavin could only battle his way aft a few inches at a time, dragging himself upward, away from the rising water.

"Gavin!" Wallace screamed.

Gavin turned to look at him. Wallace clutched the bag tightly in one hand and was barely managing to hang on with the other. "Let go of it, you fool!" Gavin shouted.

Wallace seemed not to hear him. He slipped, falling, then skidded toward the bow, tumbling over and over, scrabbling at the deck with his free hand as he slid downward. Gavin saw the bag open as Wallace rolled over once more, his arms spread wide. Silver dishes, trays, and spoons scattered across the slanting deck as Wallace screamed, falling the last fifteen feet into the water. Without a life belt, he sank almost instantly, the silver splashing into the sea after him.

Gavin wrenched around to face the stern. It was rising higher and higher, like a monster out of the sea. His breath was coming in ragged gasps as he tried to claw his way upward, away from the swirling black water.

The stern of the ship was outlined against the starry sky, and Gavin stared into the glittering night for a second, hearing the anguished screams all around him. There was a crashing roar from inside the ship, and he knew that in seconds it would sink.

He managed to drag himself forward. He grabbed the metal stanchion that held the arcing gooseneck of one lifeboat davit, then crawled, stretching to reach the next one.

Using the stanchions, Gavin worked his way upward, glancing back over his shoulder to see the dark water below him. A deck chair struck his shoulder on its way past, and he cried out, flinching, a white-hot pain in his shoulder.

Above him, the cries of terrified people mixed with the crashing sounds from inside the ship and the shrieking of stressed steel. Gavin's eyes stung from salt spray, and his hands were so cold that he could barely hold on, but still he struggled upward, ignoring the ache in his shoulder.

Gavin did not want to die. He could hear his heart hammering in rhythm with his frantic thoughts. When the ship went down, it would carry everyone still on it down with it, of that much he was sure. Somehow, he had to free himself from the *Titanic*'s enormous grasp.

Summoning all of his courage and all his remaining strength, Gavin braced his feet, then let go of the davit stanchion and sprang outward, flinging himself into a clumsy dive. For an instant, he could see a green flare going up from one of the lifeboats. It was too far away. They were probably all too far away.

The shock of the freezing water forced the breath from his body, and he fought to swim, praying that he was swimming in the right direction. Beneath the surface of the black water, there was no way to tell right from left, or even up from down. A roiling current swept over him and dragged him along with it.

He fought the rushing water, the cold seeping through every inch of his skin. He was being pulled by the downward plunge of the *Titanic*, he was almost sure. Unable to see, breathe, even to think, he kept struggling, kept swimming.

After what seemed like a black eternity, he felt himself emerge from the heaviness of the water into the knife-sharp cold of the night air. Gasping and choking, he cleared his eyes of stinging saltwater, trying to see the ship.

A streaming shower of sparks above his head startled and horrified him. The foremost funnel had fallen free and was crashing into the sea. It was so close that he felt the water lift him as the ring-shaped waves expanded around the place where the funnel had landed.

Just beyond the funnel, he saw the stern of the *Titanic* suddenly sliding downward. The rows of lights flickered as the sea covered them. The dark water swallowed everything—the shining leaded windows, the towering funnels, and the hopeless cries of the people still aboard. Gavin had time to stare at the suddenly empty ocean. Then the surging water pulled him under once more.

Gavin managed to drag in a breath before the icy water closed over his head. He didn't go straight down this time. Instead, he found himself spinning, caught in a fantastic, eddying current. He fought to free himself from the swirling tentacles of water, but this time his strength was waning. Finally, almost exhausted, he felt the ocean calming, releasing him.

He managed to break the surface at last, gasping for air again. He tipped his head to let the water drain from his ears, and raked his hair back out of his eyes, dragging in one jagged breath, then another.

Across the ink-dark ocean, Gavin heard a nightmarish screaming, the joined misery and fear of hundreds of voices. How many were in the icy water? How long would it take for the boats that had launched half full to go back for them? He spit out a mouthful of saltwater, straining to see in the darkness.

Without meaning to, he shouted, knowing that the lifeboats were too far away for anyone to hear him. Gavin fought to keep his head above the surface as he listened to the awful screaming. His legs and arms seemed heavy, clumsy. He was so cold.

"Let go before you swamp us, you idiot!"

The voice was so distinct, so clear, that Gavin jumped as though someone had touched him. He turned in the water. Which direction had the voice come from? He waited what seemed like hours before he heard more.

"Careful, Mr. Gracie, that's my foot."

Gavin's heart swelled with hope at the argumentative tone in the voice. These men didn't sound like they were drowning; they didn't sound afraid. Gavin began to swim.

The water was littered with wreckage. Gavin passed other swimmers, some of them using deck chairs for floats. One man lay flat on a door, paddling with his hands. Gavin swam past them all, stubbornly following the direction the voice had come from.

When he first saw the boat looming out of the darkness, Gavin had to squint, then blink, trying to make sense out of what he was seeing. He was almost alongside before he realized that the boat, one of the collapsibles, was overturned. Sitting, standing, kneeling, men were clinging to it, struggling to stay afloat any way they could.

"Is there room for one more?" Gavin called out, trying to keep the desperation out of his voice.

There was a silence. Then a man yelled back, "Sure, boy. Come on up."

Gavin swam close to the cork fender of the lifeboat, relieved when three or four men reached down to haul him up out of the water. He lay down, face first, shaking and coughing for a long time.

Lying still, Gavin felt the boat tilt a little as a few more men were dragged onto the awkward, overturned canvas hull. Finally, he heard the men around him explaining to swimmers that there was no more room—that they could not come aboard. Shivering and weak, Gavin sat up. He heard someone giving orders. Using splintered boards and pieces of deck chairs, the men were trying to move the overturned boat out of the reach of the desperate swimmers.

"Hold on to what you have, old boy," someone called out apologetically. "One more aboard will sink us all."

Gavin heard the answer from the swimmer. "All right, boys. Good luck and God bless you."

Gavin felt tears, unexpectedly hot, rising to fill his eyes. He could see a number of men in the water close to the boat, but the makeshift paddles were leaving them behind. Too exhausted to do more than cry, Gavin leaned to one side. The men around him had moved into the space where he had been lying down. He rested his arms on his knees and tried to weep quietly.

"This one is dead," Gavin heard someone say softly from the other side of the lifeboat. "He was in the water too long."

"Slide him off if you're sure," a voice answered. There was a small splash, then silence.

Gavin closed his eyes and prayed.

CHAPTER FOURTEEN

After an eternity, the screaming stopped and the ocean was silent and empty. Karolina stared out into the moonless night, longing for the warm amber lights of the ship. The people around her had stopped praying. They had stopped talking. Almost everyone sat hunched against the incessant cold. Not even the intermittent flares from the other lifeboats made them look up anymore. Karolina's skirt had gotten wet somehow, and she could feel the cloth stiffening as it froze.

"What was that?"

Karolina didn't bother to open her eyes, but she listened for the answer.

"Maybe it was thunder."

Karolina felt her heart shrink a little smaller. A storm was coming?

"Look at that! It's a light." Then the voice quieted. "Maybe it's just a star."

"No," the woman who sat next to Karolina disagreed. "It is a light."

Karolina sat up straight, following the woman's gesture. Another lifeboat? They had seen one or two with dim little lanterns. As she watched, a second light appeared, then a third. This one was smaller—it was *green*.

The booming sound came again, and everyone in the boat stirred, trying to see. "That's a cannon," one of the crewmen said in a prayerful voice. "It's a ship. We're saved."

Karolina strained to see the lights. Within a few minutes, it was easy to see the lighted outline of the big steamer that came toward them—and the flaring rockets fired from its deck. It slowed as it got closer. Officer Boxhall sent up a green rocket, and the steamer came straight for them.

"Shut down your engines and take us

aboard," Officer Boxhall shouted out as it got close. "I have only one sailor."

"All right," came the response from the ship.

Karolina sat still, fighting the urge to laugh aloud, to burst into tears. Why hadn't they come sooner?

"The *Titanic* has gone down with everyone onboard," a woman called out to the ship, and Officer Boxhall told her to be silent. Then they began the process of coming alongside.

It took a long time to maneuver close to the ship. Once their boat was in position, the crew above took over. They extended a rope ladder, then another long rope that was fashioned into a rough sling.

Karolina sat shivering as, one by one, they were brought up the ladder. The woman in front of her slipped and dangled for a moment over the icy water. Then the crew above hauled on the safety line and brought her aboard.

Karolina tried to climb the ladder when it was her turn, but her hands were so numb with cold that her fingers wouldn't open. A sailor helped her untie the rope harness.

"Welcome to the *Carpathia*, Miss," he said politely. "There is hot soup and coffee in the dining room. He pointed, and Karolina started away from him, the two words floating like dreams in her mind. Coffee. Soup. She heard a cry and glanced back, still walking in tiny, stiff-kneed steps. A woman had fallen onto the deck. Karolina saw two crewmen pick her up, heard a man giving orders. Then the lights of the dining room engulfed her, and she went inside.

Half an hour later, Karolina stood where she could see the ladder, her hands wrapped around a mug of broth. Trembling, she waited, staring eagerly at every pale survivor. When Aunt Rose was helped aboard, Karolina cried out and dropped the mug, running forward.

"You're all right," Aunt Rose sobbed, reaching out to gather Karolina in her arms. "They told me to get on, that there would be room for everyone. And I believed them." She held Karolina at arm's length, her eyes streaming with tears. "Then we saw how many were left on the deck. I thought you—"

"I'm fine," Karolina assured her. "I was afraid for you."

Aunt Rose was shuddering with cold as Karolina led her toward the dining room. Once her aunt had been settled in a warm chair and wrapped with blankets, Karolina went back up on deck.

The *Carpathia* was not small, but it seemed tiny compared to the *Titanic*. As survivors were brought aboard, the decks became crowded. Heading back toward the bow, Karolina saw Emily. Both her children were all right, but her own face was deathly pale. Karolina embraced Emily, then let the women surrounding her lead her off for soup and rest.

Grimly, Karolina pushed back through the crowd. It was beginning to get light now, and when she got to the rail and could see out across the water, she caught her breath. It was beautiful. The dark blue water was studded with icebergs as far as she could see. Some were very small. Others towered above the surface. The rising sun stained them muted blues and roses. She could see only two lifeboats still on the water.

*   *   *

Gavin tried to keep moving, tried to battle the creeping numbness in his feet and legs. They had lost two more men to the cold. Second Officer Lightoller had decided to keep these two bodies with them.

Gavin tried not to let his thoughts wander too far. Images of his mother kept drifting into his mind, and of his brothers and sisters. Conor would be devastated if Gavin died trying to come to America. It had been Conor's idea, after all. He kept thinking about Karolina, too. Was she as sick with cold and despair as he was? Had her boat made it away, or been caught in the ugly currents that had pulled him under? He hadn't even asked her if she could swim.

Sometime in the middle of the night, the little boat they had clung to started to sink. Officer Lightoller explained that the canvas was leaking after so long in the water. Gavin, who had begun to think that he would live, decided once more that he was probably going to die.

Lightoller snapped at them. "All right, boys, all together. Boat ahoy!" He paused, then counted to three. "Boat AHOY!" they all shouted. He counted once more, and they shouted out the words in unison, louder. "BOAT AHOY!"

There was no response. Later that endless night, a little swell rocked the boat. Some of the air trapped beneath it escaped, and it sank a little lower in the water.

"Stand up," Lightoller instructed them. "And do exactly as I say, or we'll capsize."

Gavin got unsteadily to his feet. Several of the men swayed, but managed to stay upright. "Form two lines," Lightoller ordered them. For the next eternity, they leaned first one way, then the other, following Lightoller's instructions, barely managing to keep their upside-down craft afloat.

When the sky finally lightened, someone spotted four lifeboats lashed together, not too far off. Lightoller pulled a whistle from his pocket and managed to signal them.

Gavin ended up in lifeboat number twelve. It was packed, but he welcomed the warmth of the other bodies. Lightoller had taken over command of this boat, and Gavin wanted to tell everyone that he was a good leader, that they'd had a much better chance with him aboard than they'd had before. But somehow, he had no strength to talk.

"There's a ship!" Gavin heard someone whisper as the dawn lightened the sky. A few minutes later, they all knew it was true.

Gavin felt a foggy sleep tugging at his mind and he barely heard Lightoller ordering people to stand in the stern—in order to raise the bow. As the men made their way aft, Gavin looked over the side of the boat. There were so many aboard that the bow was just inches above the waterline.

They rowed slowly toward the ship. Twice, waves broke over their bow, and the boat nearly foundered. Gavin helped bail with his hands, his fingers stiff and painful. He prayed almost constantly. He wasn't sure he'd be able to swim at all if he were dumped into the ocean now.

The ship had rope ladders hanging over the side. Her name was painted in bold letters. CARPATHIA. Gavin stared at the word. The name meant nothing to him, but it was the most lovely and graceful ship he had ever seen. Its bulk protected their little boat from the rising waves, and they made fast alongside.

Gavin needed a hand climbing the ladder, but once he was aboard, he waved off the people who seemed so eager to help him. He blinked his aching eyes. The sun seemed too bright, painful.

"There's food and blankets down that way," a man said, pointing. Gavin nodded gratefully and began to walk. His legs and feet were cramped, like unwieldy stilts made of wood.

"Gavin!"

At first he was afraid that he had imagined her voice. But when he turned, he saw Karolina's smiling face. Tears ran down her cheeks as she came toward him. She hugged him carefully, as though she knew just how unsteady he felt.

Karolina took his hand and gently led him along. "You need something warm to eat, and some sleep." She smiled at him again. "Aunt Rose made it through. Emily is sick, but the doctor says she'll recover. Her children are fine."

"Lionel?" Gavin managed to mumble. Even his voice seemed frozen and brittle.

Karolina shook her head, looking down. "I haven't seen him."

Gavin almost stumbled, then he caught himself and managed to smile at her, his face aching with cold. Lionel had saved his life. He had probably saved a lot of people's lives. Had Harry made it? He clung to the hope that he would see at least one of his friends again.

"I still have your photograph," Karolina said. "Now you can give it to Conor yourself."

Gavin looked past her, out over the open water. For a second, he wasn't sure what was missing, but he knew that something was. Then he understood. The fear. He wasn't afraid of the water anymore. He knew more about how dangerous it could be than he wanted to know. But the blind terror was gone. In its place was a hollow ache. So many had died.

"We were lucky," Karolina said quietly.

He could only nod.